BLACK PLUMES

MARGERY ALLINGHAM

BLACK PLUMES

The American Reprint Company

MATTITUCK

THE quality of mercy . . .
is twice bless'd;

—*Merchant of Venice*

BLACK PLUMES

1

THE OCTOBER WIND, WHICH HAD PROM-
ised rain all day, hesitated in its reckless flight down
the moist pavements to hurl a handful of fine drops
at the windows of the drawing room in the big
Hampstead house. The sound was sharp and spiteful,
so that the silence between the two women within
became momentarily shocked, as if it had received
some gratuitous if trivial insult.

Old Mrs Gabrielle Ivory continued to watch her
granddaughter. Her eyes were bright still, as shrewd
and black as they had been on an evening nearly
seventy years before when they had refused to drop
before the stare of another dominant woman who had
sat on a little gilt throne at the first Court of the
season. Gabrielle Ivory had been quite as forceful as
Queen Victoria in her way and certainly very much
more beautiful, but now, as she sat in her high chair,
surrounded by a lacquer screen and swaddled in grey
satin, she was very old.

The girl standing on the rug before her was barely
twenty. In her severe dark suit and Paris sailor, with
her foxes dangling from her hand, she looked even
younger, yet there was a very definite likeness between them. The eldest and the youngest of the

Ivorys both had the family's beauty, the fine bones
and that expression which was sometimes called
"straightforward" and sometimes "arrogant."

"Well?" said Gabrielle. "I'm an old woman, my
dear, nearly ninety. It's not much use coming to me.
That's what you're thinking, isn't it?" Her voice was
unexpectedly clear in spite of its thinness and there
was a quiver of amusement in the final enquiry.

Frances Ivory's long narrow grey eyes flickered.
The old lady was devastatingly right, and it was not
going to be easy to explain the sense of dismay which
had crept over her at the discovery. Meyrick Ivory,
a widower who adored his mother, had brought up
his younger daughter to see the old Gabrielle as an
almost legendary figure. To his child she had always
been presented as the beloved beauty of a golden age,
a link with the great Victorians, a creature larger than
life in power and importance, so that all through these
last perturbing weeks Frances had comforted herself
with the recollection that if the worst came to the
worst, even though Meyrick himself was half across
the world, there was always Gabrielle up at Hampstead. It was hard to realise now that the moment of
appeal had come, that she was perhaps just a very
old woman, too old and too tired to be disturbed.

The tiny figure in the high chair stirred impatiently,
as if she had read her visitor's thought and was irritated by it. It was an old habit of hers which many
people had found disturbing.

"Meyrick is not expected back from China for
some time, is he?" she remarked. "How is Robert

Madrigal behaving without him? I never liked that young man. Why your insane half sister married him I cannot imagine. Not a very suitable person to be in charge of The Gallery." She gave the title the capital letters which were its due. From the early years of the last century, when her own father-in-law, the famous Philip Ivory, had first purchased the fine house off St James's and had exhibited there the collection of Gainsboroughs which had drawn a world of rank and fashion still in stocks and beavers, 39 Sallet Square had been the gallery and so it was still, with a history of wealth and prestige behind it un-equalled in Europe.

"Well?" The old woman was persistent. "How is he behaving?"

Frances hesitated. "He and Phillida are staying with me at 38, you know," she began cautiously. "It was Meyrick's idea. He wanted Robert to be near."

Mrs Ivory's narrow lips curled. The mention of the house next door to The Gallery, where she had reigned throughout her career from its heyday in the seventies right up to the *fin de siècle*, always stirred her.

"So Phillida's at 38, is she?" she said. "Meyrick didn't tell me that. You're finding it difficult to live with her, I suppose? I don't blame you. I could never abide a fool in the house even when it was a man. A silly woman is quite insufferable. What has she done now?"

"No, it's not Phillida," said Frances slowly. "No,

darling, I only wish it were." She turned away and glanced out across the room to the barren trees far over the heath. There was a great deal more to worry about than the shortcomings of her elder half sister. "Granny," she began awkwardly, realising that the words were childish and inadequate, "there's something going on."

Gabrielle laughed. It was a little tinkling sound, as gently malicious as ever it had been in the great drawing rooms of long ago.

"There always was," she said.

"Yes, I know, but this is rather different." Frances was taking the plunge. "This is deliberate malice and it's dangerous. I'm terrified of sounding melodramatic and silly but I really do think that something irrevocable may happen at any minute and something must be done to stop it. There's nobody to go to, you see. The staff at the gallery is going to pieces. You can't blame them in the circumstances . . ."

"Oh, my dear, not business." The old woman's protest contained distaste. "Leave business to men. When I was your age we thought it rather indelicate for females to understand business. That was imbecile, of course, but we were saved a lot of unpleasantness. You should marry. Phillida has no children —a mercy, of course, if there's anything in heredity —but someone must carry on. Come and talk to me about marriage, not business."

Frances stiffened. Her suspicion was founded. There was going to be no help here. She turned away.

"Robert has just told me I ought to marry Henry

Lucar," she said. It had not occurred to her that Gabrielle might recognise the name, since Meyrick would hardly have mentioned so unimportant a member of the firm to his mother. The rustle in the high chair came as a surprise therefore.

"Wasn't that the man who was rescued from Godolphin's expedition?" demanded the old lady. "I thought he was a baggageman in charge of the camels, or was it mules?"

The girl laughed in spite of herself. "Oh no, darling," she said. "Be fair. He did go out as Robert's batman, as a matter of fact, but that's nothing to do with it. He came back a hero and he's in the firm now. I don't like him. Since Daddy's been away I've liked him less. He was always a bit of a smart aleck but just lately he's surpassed himself, cocky little beast. Still, it really isn't snobbery that's made me go on turning him down. I wouldn't care what he was if I liked him. I just don't, that's all."

She was speaking defensively, repeating the argument she had used to Robert at that astonishing interview just before lunch, and she stood squarely on the leopard rug, looking surprisingly brave and modern in the big room which was so cluttered with forgotten elegancies.

Gabrielle sat up. Marriage was a subject which her generation had entirely understood, and her bright eyes were hard.

"Did this person have the impudence to ask you to marry him?" she enquired.

Frances writhed. The *démodé* snobbery embarrassed her. It was so like great age to get the whole thing out of perspective and to pounce upon a single aspect.

"There was nothing impudent about it, darling," she protested. "It was only that when Robert began to badger me to take the horrid little brute seriously I added it to these other more serious things that have been happening and I got the wind-up. You can't blame Lucar for merely asking. Why shouldn't he?"

"Why?" Mrs Ivory sat very stiffly, the grey lace scarf over her head hanging in graceful lines by her withered cheeks. "Don't be a fool, girl, and don't forget yourself. This man Lucar is a servant, or was a servant until a gratuitous piece of good fortune saved his life and made him notorious. You are a pretty, well-bred, well-educated girl with a great deal of money. It is a ridiculous modern affectation to pretend to disregard money. It does not deceive anybody. No one thinks of anything else at heart. Your mother left you two hundred thousand pounds. That is a fortune. Of course it's impudence for the man Lucar to ask you to marry him. Any man who proposes to you is going to be in an embarrassing position unless he is either very wealthy himself or has some special advantage which makes the exchange fair and respectable. This camel man is presuming. Don't, for heaven's sake, sentimentalise over him or flatter yourself that he is anything else. Robert appears to be out of his mind. I shall certainly speak to Meyrick when he returns."

She lay back, closing her eyes after the effort, and the girl stood looking at her, her cheeks flaming. A great deal has been written about the forthrightness of the moderns shocking the Victorians, but there is no shock like the one which the forthrightness of the Victorians can give a modern.

Frances came away.

Meyrick's Rolls had never seemed more comfortingly magnificent than it did as she climbed into it out of the irritating wind which snatched at her hat and whipped at her knees. The interview had been worse than useless, and she reproached herself for attempting it. She glanced out of the window at the wet streets and huddled more closely into the corner of the car. She was frightened. That discovery was alarming in itself. It is one thing to go on from day to day with a growing feeling of unrest and suspicion, but quite another to find oneself suddenly convinced of serious trouble and to be in charge, especially when one is not quite twenty and one is alone.

The chauffeur drew up outside 38, but she signalled to him not to ring. If Phillida was still there the chances were that she was still in bed with drawn blinds and her latest medico in attendance.

She left the car and walked on down to The Gallery, which opened austere arms to greet her. At first blush 39 Sallet Square, where one could negotiate anything from a castleful of Rembrandts to a humble modern woodcut, was a cool and lovely private house. At the moment, however, the normal elegance of the building was ruffled. The girl, who was already apprehensive, noticed the changed atmosphere as soon as she set foot in the hall. Most normally sensitive people admit to some such experience, for a house where violent emotions are being stirred seems to have a flavour, a sort of restlessness in its very air, and that afternoon as Frances crossed the threshold it came down to meet her like a wave.

2

"OF COURSE. IT'S A SERIOUS THING AND naturally Mr Field is furious."

Miss Dorset leaned back in her chair in the secretary's office and her thin face flushed.

"What painter wouldn't be angry if he was rung up by a gallery in the middle of an exhibition and calmly told that one of his best pictures had been slashed? Oh, Miss Ivory, I do wish your father was back."

She was one of those thin women who had once been sandy and she had grown old in the service of the firm without anyone noticing it, not even herself. Now, as she pushed back her notes and prepared to rise, her lips were unsteady.

"Is David Field here?" Frances' tone betrayed her, but the other woman was in no mood to notice it.

"Of course he is. They're all up in Mr Meyrick's office talking it over, making a fuss and giving Mr Field something to tell everyone in London. If Mr Meyrick was here he'd explode. Formby's story has made everything only too clear, and a very dreadful thing it is too. It's that big portrait of the Mexican dancer, number sixty-four. It's a very fine picture."

"I don't understand. Did Formby see who did it?"

Frances was bewildered. Formby, the commission-
aire, had been with the firm for years and it seemed
hardly possible that any such unparalleled active
violence could have taken place under his nose.

Miss Dorset did not look at her. "He sticks to his
story," she said reluctantly. "He insists that everything was all right at two o'clock when he went into
the big gallery to speak to Mr Robert, who was there
talking to Mr Lucar. When they came out about
fifteen minutes later he went back again and found
the damage. He gave the alarm and North phoned
Mr Field. It's just like all the other outrages, malicious, dangerous and obvious."

"Does Formby actually say that nobody else was
in there except Robert and Lucar, and that they were
together? Does he see what that means?"

"Don't ask me." Miss Dorset's suppressed agitation lent her a certain defiant rakishness. "In my
life I've learnt to hold my tongue and shut my eyes
to all kinds of things in business, but now I'm beginning to wonder if discretion hasn't got a limit. I've
worked for your father since I was seventeen and I've
got a great respect for him. I've been making up my
mind to go out of my place and write the truth to him
ever since the Royal Catalogue affair. Now I'm not
so sure that I ought not to send a cable. This is a
very wonderful old firm with a great tradition and
it's a shame to see it floundering in the hands of a
lunatic, if he's nothing worse. I've never said such an
indiscreet thing in all my life, but it's the truth and
someone's got to say it."

Frances went slowly upstairs. The door to Meyrick's private office was open, and as she paused in
the corridor she could hear the voices within. She
recognised the sturdy obstinacy of the commission-
aire's polite cockney.

"Ah, but I looked at it most particularly, sir," he
was saying. "It was quite all right when I came by at
two o'clock. That I'll take my dying oath to. I should
say the same in a court of law. I can't speak fairer
than that, can I?"

"No, you can't, old boy. You've made yourself
perfectly clear. And so what? Can your people downstairs repair the thing, Madrigal? How long are they
likely to be about it?"

The second voice was not unexpected and Frances
was irritated to find herself jolted by it. David Field
was reputed to jolt a great many women in his casual,
friendly passage through life. She went forward
briskly, but the heavy carpet deadened her footsteps
and she stood on the threshold unobserved.

The white-panelled room, once an eighteenth-
century duchess' boudoir, looked odd with Robert
sitting behind the big desk and Lucar lounging idly
by his side. Of all the unprepossessing people she had
ever met Frances was inclined to give Lucar first
place. He was a pip-squeak of a man, inclined already
to fatness, with red hair and a red face which clashed
with it. Yet even these defects might have been
tolerable had it not been for his conceit. Lucar's conceit was a visible thing. It oozed from him like an
essence, tipping up his nose, quirking his mean

mouth, and clothing his shoulders and the stance of his plump little legs with a veritable aroma of perkiness. He alone of the group looked perfectly pleased with himself. Robert was even more nervy than usual. His coffin-shaped face was grey, he was punching small holes in the blotting paper with a dry pen, and his hand was shaking.

Formby was standing solidly with his back to her, and in the armchair beside him there was a tall thin figure at whom Frances did not look. She was not given to shyness in the ordinary way but she did not glance at David Field.

"Don't worry, Mr Field. We'll patch it up for you." It was Lucar who spoke, and his jauntiness was insulting. "It may be out of the show for a day or two, but there you are. It can't be helped, can it?"

Robert cut in at once. "You can rely on us absolutely. We shall see to it immediately," he said hastily. "I can't tell you how shocked and horrified we all are that such an accident should have occurred to such a fine picture when it was in our care."

"You're insured, of course?" Field put the question absently and an awkward pause ensued.

"Yes, we are, naturally. Fully." There were unaccustomed spots of colour in Robert's cheeks. "Naturally. But in this particular circumstance, I mean in view of the slightness of the damage, I think a claim would hold up the repair work unnecessarily. After all, we do want the canvas on show, don't we? That's the main thing."

It was a bad cover up and very obvious. Field rose

and his lean figure was silhouetted against the light.

"Ye-es, I suppose so," he said, regarding them, his head slightly on one side. "Look here, Madrigal, exactly what sort of accident was it?"

It was an invitation to frankness typical of the man, yet Robert did not avail himself of it. He looked up, and his deep-set eyes, which could cloud with fury at the least irritation, were disconcertingly blank.

"I have no idea," he said stiffly. "No idea at all."

The painter shrugged his shoulders. "Oh, all right," he said. "I'm probably a fool, but get it repaired and back in its place by the end of the week and we'll forget the incident. But meanwhile, for the love of Mike, do look after the stuff. Meyrick Ivory was a good friend to me when I was beginning, and I don't want to hurt the old man, but these things are painted in blood and sweat. I can't let 'em be carved up indiscriminately. One more disaster and we'll have to call the show off."

Lucar opened his mouth. He had a curious self-conscious wriggle of the shoulders before making one of his more unforgivable utterances and fortunately Robert saw it coming.

"Quite," he said quickly. "Quite. North is upstairs now arranging for it to be taken down. Perhaps you would go up to him, Lucar. Impress it on him that he must take every possible care. It's a terrible thing to have happened, terrible."

There was nervous tension in every word and Lucar shrugged his shoulders. He slid off the edge of the

desk where he had been sitting and, turning towards
the door, caught sight of Frances.

"Why, it's Miss Ivory," he said, giving the name
an unction which was both arch and insulting.
"That's cheered up my afternoon. Mind you, wait.
I'll be down in a minute." He flashed a meaning smile
at her and bounced out, leaving them all uncomfortable.

"Hello, Frances." Robert forced an unconvincing
smile. "You've met Mr Field, haven't you?"

"I should hope so." The painter sprang up. "She
was my first client. I painted her when she was fourteen. The fee Meyrick paid me got me into the U.S.
Hence my career. Hallo, Frances love, I'm very de-
pressed. Someone's been sticking knives into my
beautiful señorita. It's the insult that gets one down.
Madrigal doesn't appreciate that. What are you doing now? Come out and have a sherry. Or is it out of
hours? I can't get used to my home town again after
years of freedom. Well, never mind, let's go and eat
ice cream."

He was talking to relieve her from any embarrassment which Lucar's reception might have afforded
her and she was grateful.

"There's nothing I'd like better," she said honestly.

"Fine. We'll go now before Little Consequential
returns, shall we?" The sneer was a very gentle one,
considering, and she was surprised at his restraint.
Most people's pet names for Lucar were less polite.

Robert cleared his throat. "I didn't think you'd be

going out, Frances," he said. The words came haltingly and with so much suppressed irritation behind them that they turned to stare at him. Frances caught the message in his eyes and was indignant. He was actually ordering her to stay because Lucar had expressed a wish to see her.

"Oh, but I am," she said firmly. "I don't get a sound offer of ice cream every day. Shall we go now?"

She held out her hand to Field impulsively, and he took it at once and tucked her arm through his.

"I painted her licking an ice-cream cornet," he remarked, grinning at Robert. "The sticky highlights round the chin were masterly. Where is that picture, by the way?"

"In Meyrick's bedroom." Frances spoke absently and added with an ingenuousness which she knew to be undignified, "Oh, do come on."

"Poor woman, she's starving," said Field. "Righto, ducky. D'you think you can bear up until we get across the road?"

He swept her out of the room, still laughing, and they left Robert standing behind the desk, his shaking hands resting on the blotting paper.

Looking back on that scene in the long, terrifying days to follow Frances Ivory was to wonder how much might have been altered, how much disaster averted, had they stayed beside him.

3

THEY WENT TO THE CAFÉ ROYAL, WHICH
was practically deserted at that hour of the day, and
as Frances played with the sundae she did not want
she considered Field afresh. At fourteen she had decided that he filled the somewhat exacting require-
ments of her ideal man. He had been younger then
than she had supposed, and now it occurred to her
that the seven years between twenty-five and thirty-
two had not altered him particularly. He still had the
fine head with the sensitive, almost ascetic features,
which were contradicted by his expression which was
both lazy and sophisticated. There was no grey in
his dark hair, and his square painter's hands were
hard and full, like a boy's.

"What's going on at your place?" He put the
question casually and seemed surprised when she
avoided his glance.

"How do you mean?" she said defensively.

He stirred and she knew he was smiling, with his
mouth drawn down at the corners.

"You don't want to talk about it. All right. I
rather got the impression you did. Sorry. We'll talk
about string."

"Why? Did you notice anything?" She realised

that the question was absurd as soon as she had put it and he laughed.

"I did, as a matter of fact," he said. "Either Phillida's husband or that painful little excrescence with the ginger hair stuck a penknife into one of my best paintings. You may feel it's negligible, but it's not the sort of treatment your poor papa would give a canvas he was commissioned to sell, or at least I don't think so unless times have changed while I've been staggering round God's own country. I may be wrong, too, but I thought you were in a spot of trouble yourself. My dear child, you positively clung to me. It was most touching. Don't apologise. I liked it. My youth came rushing back with all the vine leaves and tendrils of romance. However, don't bother. Don't open up the family bone cupboard if you don't want to. But if you do here am I with nothing on hand, safe, sound and respectable, also eager to sympathise. What's up? The ginger twip has something on Robert, has he?"

"Blackmail, you mean?" Now that the word was out it did not seem quite so terrible.

"Well, I don't know." He was being cautiously casual. "I don't suppose Robert did the knifing himself, and when one chap covers up another with such desperate determination the evil thought has a way of cropping up in one's mind. It's horribly bad for business, though, that sort of thing. I'm quite remarkably easygoing, even for a painter, and I'm sitting here seething. Do you realise that?"

Frances looked at him sharply. His tone had

changed slightly and she caught him unawares. Behind his smile his round dark eyes were sincerely
furious. He caught short her stream of apology.

"I don't want that, my dear," he said. "It's nothing to do with you or your old man either. Those two
lads evidently have something on and I rather wondered what it was. That was all. Had any other
trouble?"

He made it so easy. Frances had experienced one
disastrous attempt to confide that afternoon and now
she found in him the ideal listener. She told him the
story. She described the little incident of the broken
Kang-Tse vase in the antique room, mentioned the
infuriating affair of the special catalogue prepared
for royalty only to be discovered, a heap of charred
remains, ten minutes before the august personage
was due to arrive, and sketched in the circumstances
which had led to the resignation of the invaluable
old Peterson who had been with the firm for thirty
years.

It was a curious history. The series of suspicious
incidents, each one a little more serious than the last,
made up a considerable sum of disaster, and the
underlying fear in the young voice was appealing.
He listened to her attentively.

"It's not good, old girl," he said at last. "In fact
it's damned disturbing. They're not the little petty
things which an office boy might do in a fit of in-
growing adolescence, either. The vase was darned
near priceless, I suppose? Peterson was important
and my picture might have caused a hell of a row if

I hadn't been so blessed slack. What are you going
to do? It's difficult to get Meyrick back at once, I
take it? You're all pretty sure that Ginger is the
man?"

"Oh yes, I think so." Frances spoke soberly and
afterwards she shivered a little as an unbidden
thought crept into her mind. He noticed the gesture
immediately. He was amazingly sensitive to her least
reaction, she realised, and put it down to his vast and
notorious experience.

"Who is he?" he enquired. "Where did he come
from?"

She began to explain, and a light of comprehension
passed over his face.

"Dolly Godolphin's Tibetan expedition? The secret climb through the Himalayan pass?" he said. "I
read about that at the time. Wonderfully exciting.
They were very interested in it in the States. All the
papers reported it. Robert and Lucar were the only
two to return, were they? Oh well, that accounts for a
lot. Ginger probably saved Robert's life or something.
That show was a sporting effort all round. All kinds
of people might have thought up a project like that,
but no one but Godolphin could possibly have persuaded a tough old nut like Meyrick to finance him.
Robert went as 'Art Adviser,' if I remember? I bet
that was Meyrick's idea. I can hear him insisting that
Dolly take someone who could tell a valuable from
a mere curio. I can't exactly see Robert on an adventure like that, though. It's odd, isn't it? It always
is the rabbit who returns while the lion is left to

bleach in the sun. Godolphin was an extraordinary chap. He would have revelled in your present situation, by the way. You knew him, of course?"

She nodded. "I saw quite a lot of him in the school holidays during my last year. He and Phillida ran round together quite a bit."

"So they did." His eyes were wide and amused. "Your half sister believed in numbers."

Frances looked at him briefly. It had been true, then. Phillida had always added Field to her list of conquests but there was never any guarantee with Phillida's reminiscences. Field, then, and Godolphin and half a dozen others; they had all been in love with Phillida, who had forgotten them for a string of imaginary ailments and who had married in the end Robert, of all people. It seemed to Frances that the older she grew the more extraordinary life became.

"Robert stuck," she said slowly, continuing her thought aloud. "The others drifted away and Godolphin got lost in Tibet, but Robert stuck. He's got a sort of character under all that nerviness, you know. There's a sort of determination about him which is almost terrifying. He gets his own way if it's only by sticking to his point long after everyone is exhausted. That's why I'm so stupidly afraid, I suppose."

David picked her up. "That's a strong word," he said. "Why afraid? I didn't know people of your age were ever anything so undignified."

"Robert wants me to marry Lucar," she said frankly, "and although I know it's absurd he has such

an uncanny way of getting what he wants that I
sometimes feel that I might go mad and do it."

He caught her expression and his eyebrows rose.

"Ginger?" he demanded. "This isn't serious, is it?
I shouldn't stand for that. That's damned insulting.
Robert's nuts, of course."

His unusual vehemence was comforting and she
grinned at him.

"He's such a little tick," she said and he nodded.

"He makes himself a bit of a nuisance, I suppose?
That type can. They're the only specimens left alive.
The women seem to have got the rest of us to heel,
but that thick-skinned bumptious breed can make
themselves a blot on the landscape for years. They're
unsnubbable. You don't like to go off to the South, of
course, because of the trouble, I suppose? Yes, well
that's not good, Frances my love. You're in a mess."

She smiled at him wryly. It was very comforting
and pleasant to be in his company. He had ease and
friendliness and, above all, that curious sophisticated
sympathy which made talking to him a Rolls-Royce
affair.

"You'd better get engaged," he said. "That 'll
scotch all that nonsense until Meyrick returns. Be-
trothal is old fashioned, I know, but it has its virtues,
like flannel. Any likely lad about?"

She laughed. "No one I could ask," she said.

He did not seem to be particularly amused. "It
ought to be someone you know or it might lead to
marriage," he said seriously. "When's your father
due home?"

"January or February."

"A long time. Phillida's just her own sweet self, I take it?"

"Just about.".

"Oh. Well, suppose I take you out now and buy you a ring? Not a violently expensive one, but decent enough to show the relations. Any good?"

He had lost a great deal of his lightheartedness, and it flashed through her mind that he was embarrassed. She was astounded. David Field had one of those curious reputations which are based on no concrete fact, that is to say, although he was reputed to be a lion among women there were no actual names with which his own was linked. There had been no marriages, no divorces, no engagements. No one remembered any actual affair of any duration.

He was watching her face and she reddened guiltily.

"I'm not asking you to marry me and I don't suppose we ever should," he said with an abruptness which was unlike him. "I mean even if we became hysterical about each other—and that sort of thing does happen, you'd be surprised—there's the question of money. I'm very sensitive about money. I make a bit, quite enough to feed a healthy female, but I'm not outrageously rich and I never shall be. You've got an indecent amount of cash. That rather rules out marriage, you see. My blessed child, don't look at me like that. I know I'm insane on the subject. I wish I wasn't. It's a phobia with me. I was once accused of being a fortune hunter and I damned nearly killed the old woman who suggested it. I had

an Indian club in my hand at the time—honestly,
this is no laughing matter—and I raised it. I didn't
hit her, thank God, but I was going to. I felt it. I've
never been more frightened in my life. My hat, that
was a near thing!"

He sat back and it dawned on her that he was not
entirely joking. His smile had vanished, and for an
instant she saw determination in his eyes and a half-
frightened, half-passionate honesty.

"So marriage is off," he resumed cheerfully, "unless, of course, you could see your way to a large-scale
hospital endowment scheme, and I shouldn't do that
for a bit because, you never know, we might not get
on. However, joking apart, I don't go back to New
York until April, and meanwhile if you'd care for an
engagement ring let's go out and buy one."

Frances remained silent. She was not even sure if he
was serious. On the face of it the proposition was a
wild one but it was attractive. Meanwhile he continued to regard her quizzically, his eyes half shut,
his mouth drawn down in its familiar smile, and she
wondered if he was laughing at her. As it happened,
he was merely considering her with the dispassionate
curiosity of the professional painter. He saw that the
fine bones which he had painted five years before
were now more apparent and that the slightly up-
ward line of the long narrow eyes, which had so delighted him when he first discovered it, had become
accentuated. She was lovely, nor was it, he thought,
the *beauté du diable*. When Frances Ivory was as old
as Gabrielle she would still have strength and breed-

ing in her shapely head, character and sensitiveness
in her wide mouth.

"Well?" he said.

"It would settle one of my difficulties until Meyrick comes home, but it seems a frightful imposition."
She made the announcement dubiously and was then
unreasonably dashed because he did not protest.

"Anything to oblige an old client," he said lightly.
"That's a bet, then. We'll buy the ring, write the
newspapers and go and tell the family. Ginger can
bite his fingernails and Robert can lay off the match-
making. That 'll be one embarrassment settled.
When the time comes you can throw me over for another or we can quarrel about the ballet, which is a
nice refined thing to do. Meanwhile stick to the story.
That's the main thing."

She hung back awkwardly.

"You won't be upsetting anybody?" she enquired
at last. "Any other woman, I mean."

"I? Oh lord, no, I'm free, unattached and un-
beloved." He laughed at her expression. "I'm doing
you a signal honour in entrusting you with my
precious liberty. I hope you realise that! I'm banking
on your nice bringing-up. I've never even been engaged before. The old man is a frightful cad at heart.
He always slithers out of it in the end. None of the
objects of my adoration has ever got her hooks in me."

"Why? Was it always money?"

He frowned. "Eh?" he said. "Oh yes, money.
That and other things. Come on, you'll have to have
an aquamarine with those eyes."

They were laughing again as they stepped into the street, and the fitful wind plucked at their sleeves and threw warm, soft rain in their eyes, tormenting them, beseeching their attention. Afterwards they both remembered it. As they went over each incident in that fateful day the motif of the squalling wind kept recurring like the thin blast of a warning trumpet, but they were deaf to it and went on their predestined way unaware.

4

"WHERE ARE THEY NOW? IN THE GARDEN room? Oh, Frances, how could you do this? How could you?"

Phillida Madrigal lay among the lace-covered cushions on her day bed and wept in the firelight.

"It's the strain, the intolerable strain," she whispered. "Every little hideous sound sends a network of pain all over me. Wasn't it enough for me to be annihilated by the impossible scene with Gabrielle without you rushing in and starting another with Robert and David Field?"

Frances stood on the hearthrug of the white-panelled bedroom. It was typical of Phillida to behave like this after a row which had been nothing to do with her, she reflected.

"I had no idea that Granny had come here, let alone that she was still in the house," she said, twisting the new ring round her finger. "It never occurred to me that she might actually drive out and tackle Robert. She's so terrifyingly old. I didn't think she understood a word I said this afternoon."

"Oh, she understood." Mrs Phillida Madrigal forgot her tears in her anger. "She's as strong as a horse and as obstinate as a mule. I wish to God I had her

26

strength. When she came in on old Dorothea's arm she positively dominated the entire house. Robert was mad to be rude to her. That was sheer idiocy. I stood there with my heart racing, which means I shall be a rag tomorrow. She listened to him, she let him rage, she let him say the most unforgivable things, and then she simply sat down and sent Dorothea out to prepare Meyrick's bedroom for her. Naturally Robert protested—I did myself. How can she stay here? Is it reasonable? She was utterly obstinate. She said it had been her room for thirty years and she was going to bed in it. What could one do? There was nothing to say. I thought Robert was going to faint. He looked like a death's-head. Finally Dorothea took her up. Gabrielle ignored Robert. She simply looked through him. But she had heard what he said. She's dangerous, Frances. A hard, selfish, proud old woman. And she's in the house. It's your fault. You may have killed her. You may have started up anything. Oh, don't you think you ought to go down?"

She was sitting up now, and the faint light was kind to her, taking out the petulant lines round her mouth and deepening the shadows round her eyes, burnishing the copper lights in her smooth hair.

"Do go down to those two, Frances."

"How can I?" The younger girl spoke wearily. "Robert said he wanted to talk to David alone. He could hardly have made himself more clear."

Phillida got up and walked down the room, her lace negligee trailing on the dark carpet.

"Frances," she said suddenly and with more force in her voice than her half sister had ever suspected it could contain, "have you ever thought that Robert might be mad?"

The question would have been remarkable if only because it came from Phillida and concerned the state of mind of somebody other than herself, but up in the dark bedroom, with the firelight flickering and the wind chattering round the house, its very directness shot a chill to Frances' diaphragm.

"Why? Why do you say that?"

"Oh, nothing. I'm nervy. I'm ill. I'm frightened. I hate this insufferable house. I've only been married to him two years, Frances. He's always been queer and difficult, but just lately he's much much worse. He's getting worse every day. He watches me, he watches you. He doesn't talk to anyone except Lucar. He's made up his mind that you shall marry Lucar."

"Then I'm afraid he's doomed to disappointment, my dear."

Phillida did not answer for some minutes, and when at last she spoke her remark was unexpected.

"Did you know that David Field had a dreadful row with Gabrielle once over me? It was years ago, of course, long before he became known." She laughed abruptly and threw up her arms in a sudden gesture. "Oh, why did I marry Robert?" she said. "Why out of all of them did I marry Robert? It's obvious how it happened. I was secretly engaged to Dolly Godolphin when they went out on that ghastly expedition, and then when poor Dolly was lost and I was brokenhearted Robert just happened to be there. I was mad. Oh, Frances, be careful who you marry."

She went back to the day bed and, throwing herself down upon it, began to cry so quietly that the other girl did not hear her. Frances was staring into the fire. So it had been Gabrielle who had called him a fortune hunter and raised the devil in him. How like him not to have mentioned it.

Phillida's muffled voice cut into her thoughts with a startling suggestion.

"For God's sake go down to them. What can they possibly be *doing* all this time? They've both got insane tempers. Go down and see."

Frances looked up sharply. "Perhaps I'd better," she said and found that her breath was uneven.

Just outside the door she ran into Dorothea, Gabrielle's elderly maid. The plump old woman was pale with unaccustomed excitement and she laid a hand on the girl's arm.

"I can't do a thing with her," she said in the sickroom whisper she always adopted when speaking of her mistress. "She won't go to bed and she won't take any drops. She's sitting up in the armchair, staring round the room and talking of the late master and Mr Meyrick. He didn't ought to have said those things to her, Mr Robert didn't. She wouldn't have stood it from one of her own and she certainly won't from him. She's angry, that's what she is. I've only seen her like it twice before in my life, once when Mr Meyrick's first wife, Miss Phillida's mother, ran off and left him, and once when she had some words

with a young gentleman who came to the house.
She's angry and she's old. She's brooding. I wondered
should I send for a doctor."

"I don't see what he could do, do you?" said
Frances. "I'm afraid all this is my fault, Dorothea.
I'm so sorry."

The old woman regarded her with the stern common sense of her kind.

"Well, it hasn't done a lot of good, has it, miss?"
she said. "I'll wait a bit and see how she is later. I'll
go down in a minute and get her a mite of hot milk.
She may take that and go to sleep. He *has* upset her.
Someone ought to tell him of it. He might have killed
her. They make me wild, these nervy men. There's
something very wrong in this house. I notice it if you
don't. Something very wrong."

She went off down the corridor, a solid, angry old
figure diverted from her daily task and resenting it
bitterly. Frances went on downstairs. The house was
quiet and almost dark.

The garden room was at the end of the passage off
the main hall. There were two doors side by side, one
leading to the room and the other giving out onto an
iron staircase running down to the flagged yard, which
was all that encroaching London had left of an
eighteenth-century rosary.

At the mouth of the corridor she hesitated. A man
was hurrying down it towards her. To her astonishment she recognised Lucar. She was so surprised to
find him in the house at that time of night that she
did not move, and he came up with her. She saw

at once that something had happened to him. He was
shaking with fury and his red face was patched with
white where taut muscles had banished the blood.
Also he was smiling. He paused in front of her. His
eyes were not far above the level of her own and she
was suddenly alarmed by them. He did not speak but
remained looking at her, and she attempted to pass
him with a conventional murmur. He shot out a hand,
however, and, catching her arm, swung her round.
She was not prepared for his strength. She had assumed that because he was small he must necessarily
be a weed, but the grip on her wrist was paralysing,
and she was all but jerked off her feet. He lifted her
hand and looked for the ring on it. When he saw it he
flung her away from him and strode off down the
hall into the shadows of the porch, leaving her angry
and breathless.

She collected herself and was annoyed to find that
she was trembling, and she went on down the corridor, her courage up but her knees shaking. Outside
the door of the garden room she paused. There was
an ominous silence within, and her outstretched hand
drew away from the latch. Disliking herself for the
subterfuge, she turned to the other door and let herself out onto the iron steps. The yard was a well of
darkness. Here the wind which had roystered over
the city all day seemed to have become imprisoned,
for it tore round the high walls like a live thing,
twitching at her skirt and blowing her hair into her
eyes as it passed.

She went softly down the staircase and took a step

or two across the flags. Around her were dim forms
in the faint light from the sky where scudding clouds
raced across the moon. There was a packing case
containing one of Meyrick's Chinese purchases standing like a gun emplacement behind her, and beyond,
in the angle of the wall, was a little shed where some
of the wood for the gallery's casemaking was kept.
Frances looked up at the great bulwark of the house.
All the windows save one were in darkness, but the
curtains of the garden room had not been drawn and
she saw David distinctly. He was standing behind
the table, leaning on it and looking down. The scene
had the brilliant unreality of a stage-set. The man
was clear and she could see his face clearly. He was
not talking but might have been listening or merely
looking, and his expression was curiously blank.

It was that blankness which first terrified her, it
was so unlike him. His lazy smile might never have
existed, and his eyes were hard and apparently un-
seeing.

The moment seemed to drag out intolerably and
then, just when she was on the point of screwing up
her courage to break in on them, came the sound.

It was a little stir, a little shuffling which was not
quite the wind, and it was behind her. She swung
round, her heart rising. The shaft from the window
made a narrow angle of light which ran right across
the door of the shed, cutting it in two and passing
directly through the latch. As she turned she could
have sworn that the handle moved and the door
cracked inwards.

Panic, unreasoning and uncontrollable, descended upon her. Out in the wind-swept darkness at the bottom of that well of tall houses fear enveloped and suffocated her. She ran. She fled up the iron staircase, through the corridor, across the hall, mounted the main stairs and rushed over the upper landing into her own room.

She was still there, crouching on the dressing-table stool, trying to pull herself together and to force the terror which had seized her out of her mind, when David knocked and put his head in.

"I took a chance on finding the right door," he said, coming over to her. "Well, my dear, we're still engaged."

The words were meant to be reassuring, but he was speaking with an uncharacteristic jerkiness, and she stared at him in panic.

"What's the matter? What's happened?"

"Nothing." The denial came a little too quickly and he laughed to cover it. "I just thought I'd see you before I went, to tell you it's all okay in spite of our Robert's unendearing manners. He's going off for a walk, by the way. It's not a bad idea. The night air may cool him down a bit."

"What did he say?"

He avoided her eyes and looked over her head at the swaying curtains.

"Just about what you'd think," he said. "Forget him. We're engaged. Good night."

She thought he was going to kiss her, but either he changed his mind or the idea had not occurred to

him, for he merely touched her hand abruptly and
went out, closing the door behind him.

She stood where she was for some time and then,
on an impulse, followed him out into the upper hall.
It was quite dark and silent, and she crept forward to
lean over the balustrade. The hall below was an inky
pit, and the sound of the front door closing startled
her. She waited but there was still no light and no
sound of a returning servant, so she took it that
David had let himself out.

With his going she was overwhelmed with an inexplicable sense of loss. The familiar house, which had
been her home all her life, had suddenly become not
so much empty as hostile. Phillida's door was closed
and there was no light beneath it, nor was there any
sign of life from Meyrick's room where the old
Gabrielle must be lying in the antique Italian bed
with the tapestry hangings. It was all quiet, all dark,
all for some intangible reason menacing.

And then, while she stood there, something happened. Someone walked sharply down the corridor
from the garden room, crossed the hall with a brisk,
light step, and strode out of the house, closing the
front door firmly behind him. She saw no one. There
was not a shadow in the dusk. The sounds were so
sharp and decisive that they should have struck a
reassuring note in that world of creaks and whispers,
yet to the girl clinging to the slender balustrade
they were so horrifying that she almost screamed,
and as she crept back to the light of her own room

they sank into her mind with a vividness which she was afterwards to regard as prophetic.

"It's only Robert going out for his walk," she said aloud to herself in the mirror. "Only Robert going out, you fool." But her voice was not reassuring, and the face which looked back at her from the pool of light was white and terrified.

Yet on the following morning when Norris, Meyrick's butler, announced with the casual urbanity, which he seemed to reserve for more awkward intimations, that Mr Robert had not been in the house all night but that his hat and coat were missing, and enquired a trifle slyly if his letters had not best be sent down to his club, no one was particularly alarmed.

Relief came first: relief for Frances, relief for Phillida, relief for Gabrielle holding court in her great tapestry-hung bed.

Fear came later. It began on the third day when it was discovered that Robert was not sulking in Jermyn Street, and fear deepened and grew into dull terror when discreet enquiries at Blue Bridges, the Surrey country house, brought no news of him, and when the valet at the Paris flat wired back to say that Monsieur was not there.

Fear came with the letters to Frances, pouring in after the announcement of the engagement. Fear came with the discreet enquiries from Robert's few friends. Fear came with a hundred-and-one little demands for Robert's decision in business matters.

Fear came from Lucar's sullenness, from Phillida's

hysterics and from the odd, preoccupied expression in David's eyes.

And then one morning seven days after Robert's disappearance two things happened. One was the news, wired from the wilds of the Northwest province of India and flashed into every newspaper office in the world. The curt message appeared on the evening-paper boards as the early racing editions were piled into the streets. Phillida read them from her bedroom window as they stood propped up against the railings of the square.

GODOLPHIN SAVED

FAMOUS EXPLORER
ESCAPES FROM
FORBIDDEN
TERRITORY

She was standing there staring at the display, too petrified to throw up the window and shout for a newsboy, when the second event occurred which forced the first into obscurity, focussed the attention of the entire city on Sallet Square, and brought Meyrick racing back from China as fast as train and plane could carry him.

Frances came into her half sister's room without ceremony. She was trying to keep very quiet, very calm, and her grey eyes were dark with the effort of control.

"Phillida," she said huskily, "something's happened. You've got to pull yourself together, darling. You've got to be incredibly brave and—and—— Oh, for God's sake, keep your head."

The woman swung round. "They've found Robert?"

Frances regarded her steadily.

"Yes," she said. "Did you know?"

"I? No, of course not. I don't know anything. Where is he? What's he done?"

"Oh, darling." The young voice quivered and broke. "I'm so sorry. I didn't mean that. I don't know what I thought. He—he's been down in the garden room all the time. His coat and hat were there too, lying on top of him. That cupboard's never opened, you know. There's nothing in it in the ordinary way. They've just found him. Norris called me."

The words were tumbling out of her mouth in a helpless stream, and she struggled to restrain them.

Phillida came quietly across the room towards her. For a moment it was she who was controlled, she who was the dominating figure. She laid her hand on her half sister's shoulder and shook her.

"Frances, are you telling me that Robert is dead?"

The girl met her eyes and her own were panic-stricken. She nodded.

Phillida's hand dropped. Her face was calm and her tone rather horribly matter of fact.

"Thank God," she said simply.

5

"I SHOULDN'T COME IF I WERE YOU, madam."

The unnatural sharpness in the butler's voice and a curious new dishevelment about him which seemed to be rather of expression than of actual fact gave the words a macabre quality of their own. Frances felt Phillida waver in the crook of her arm as the two women paused abruptly in the passage outside the garden room while the man barred their path in the sharp angle of the half-closed door.

"I shouldn't come in," he repeated stubbornly, adding with sudden weakness, "he's—he's just as he was, you see. We mustn't move anything before the police come."

Phillida shook her head. It was a vigorous, meaningless movement, and in that nightmare moment when all events seemed to be moving with unnatural slowness and each familiar object, the door frame, Norris' white face and the pallid perkiness of his winged collar appeared to have broad black outlines like the pictures in a child's rag book, the gesture appeared to have a dreadful studied idiocy.

"No," said Phillida. "No. Get out of the way, Norris."

The blaze of light in the garden room in the morning always came as a surprise as one turned to it out of the cool greyness of the hall, but today its radiance was pitiless. The sunlight poured into the room through the wide-open window with the energy of a living thing. It burnt on the old green leather chair, throwing up each scar and scratch upon the livid hide. It found a speck of dust on the mahogany of the antique glass-fronted bookcase and pointed to it as if it had been a crime. Nor did it respect the deep recess behind the open door in the white panelling but hurled itself within and pounced with indecent savagery upon the dreadful thing, the thing with the mercilessly exposed head and the strange, dusty-looking hair.

Robert Madrigal had died and stiffened and grown limp again. He sat squarely in the bottom of the cupboard, his back supported by the wall and his legs doubled up before him. Across his knees lay a raincoat, a pair of yellow gloves and, final touch of ghastly incongruity, an upturned bowler hat.

Frances took Phillida's full weight as she heeled over, and Norris caught them both as they reeled against the table.

"I said not to go in. I said not to go in," he repeated infuriatingly to Frances as between them they got the other woman out into the passage. "I've phoned the police and the doctor. You take her, miss. I can't leave *him*, can I?"

Neither of them saw anything absurd in the final statement, although Robert Madrigal had been left

alone for many days and would be left alone for an
eternity, he with his coffin-shaped face and his long
parchment hands.

Old Dorothea appeared like a creature from another and a happier world. She came waddling down
the corridor from the hall where the rest of the staff
lingered in whispering conclave and put capable
nurse's hands on Phillida's elbows.

"Come along, my dear. Come along, my pretty.
Come along, my brave girl," she said, slurring all
the words together until they had no meaning but
made a single comforting sound. "And you, too, Miss
Frances," she added over her shoulder with calculated tartness. "I don't know what you think you're
doing, taking her in there, and her so delicate as it is.
Come along, my dear. Come along, my pretty. Come
along, my brave girl. One step up. Now another.
Come along. Come along."

She had the dynamic energy of the sunlight itself,
and her stalwart body moved with the magnificent
drive and precision of a little draught horse sur-
mounting a hill. Frances plodded on beside her,
supporting Phillida's other arm.

The Italian bed in Meyrick's room was an impressive erection. The baroque gilt framework rose
to the ceiling and the two movable wings hung out
on either side like banners. The bright tapestry of
the triptych had not faded and Matthew, Mark, Luke
and John blessed the couch which Gabrielle lay on in
vivid blue and gold and red.

She sat up in it, wrapped in Shetland lace, remote

and inapproachable, a little yellow scrap of dying authority. Dorothea led the procession into the room without ceremony. She lowered Phillida into a chair by the open fire and began to slap her hands with rhythmic determination.

The old Gabrielle's bright black eyes rested on the two of them for a moment and the expression on her pursed mouth was almost contemptuous. Finally she sniffed delicately, like a little wood animal, and beckoned Frances over with a finger raised among the woolly lace.

"Are the police here yet?" The old voice was brisk in spite of the lowered tone.

"No, darling."

"Nor the doctor?"

"No, not yet."

"Does the servant know how the man died?"

"No, I don't think so. I don't know."

"Go and find out and come and tell me. Hurry, child, hurry."

It was extraordinary, as if disaster had fanned a flickering fire into life again. So here was Gabrielle, a force once more albeit a fleeting and uncertain one. Frances went out.

At the head of the staircase she paused. There was movement in the hall below and the hissing of subdued voices. With sudden guiltiness she drew back and hung over the balustrade. Her heart turned over as she saw the group below. The hall was crowded. The Georgian elegance of 38 Sallet Square was in the hands of the police.

Norris was there, very much in evidence. He was whispering to a uniformed police inspector and another man, a tall, gloomy-looking stranger in a spruce tweed suit whose grizzled head was held sideways in a curious terrierlike attitude which she was to come to know very well indeed. Directly beneath her a maid hovered nervously, and behind the girl she saw the door to the service corridor was ajar. From her place of vantage she could see the housekeeper listening behind it.

The whole picture was vaguely ridiculous with its broadened angles and foreshortened figures, like some delightful Gluyas Williams absurdity with a new and terrible difference.

As she stood looking down there was a clatter on the flags as the police photographers arrived. Their strident, decisive tramp touched a memory in her mind, and her fingers gripped the polished wood.

Not so long ago she had hung over this same balustrade and had peered down into the grey darkness, and on that occasion, too, there had been sharp footsteps marching swiftly across the hall. Then it had been a sound which should have been reassuring, and her own mental admonition returned to her: "It's only Robert going out, you fool. It's only Robert going out." Robert going out? Robert going out! In view of the morning's discovery the suggestion was ghastly. Robert had not gone out that night. Robert, poor, ill-tempered, ineffectual Robert had remained in the garden room. At that moment a week ago when she had hung here listening Robert must

already have been sitting in the bottom of the big
cupboard, his head lolling and his legs twisted horribly beneath him.

Someone else had gone out. Someone else had
walked into the windy darkness with the fine rain
whipping at his ankles and folding his garments
more closely about him. Someone else. . . . Who?

There was another movement in the hall below as
a new arrival came slowly forward from the porch,
The entire company turned towards him, and Frances
felt the skin at the back of her neck tighten as she
recognised him.

She never forgot David as she saw him at that
moment. It was not that she had never known before
that she was in love with him, nor did it seem then or
afterwards that his appearance had any deep emotional significance. It was simply that he sprang to
her mind, a vivid and complete picture which never
quite faded again.

He came quietly into the room, casual and friendly
as usual, and stooping a little because of his height
and the looseness of his lean figure. He glanced round
him with the faintly surprised expression which was
half his charm and suddenly glanced up, as if he knew
where to find her, and raised his hand in friendly
salute.

Everyone stared at her and she came down hurriedly, aware that she was white and frightened and
completely demoralised by the appalling idea which
had just come to her. Norris said something to the
man with the grizzled hair who came forward to

meet her. She had no idea who he was, and even had he introduced himself it is not likely that his name or his exalted rank of divisional detective inspector would have made much impression on her at that moment, but she could not fail to recognise authority in his face nor to see in those small steady eyes that rigorous honesty which is, perhaps because of its corresponding cruelty, the most terrifying quality in the world.

"If you'll chust wait upstairs for a little, Miss Ivory, I'll send for ye in a moment or two," he said, revealing the soft voice and absence of *j*s of the Orkney Scot. There was no question in the remark; it was an order, given courteously but irrevocably, and the question which had been on her lips died before it was spoken. She nodded and glanced at David Field, but the newcomer was before her.

"You'll be Mr Field, won't ye?" he was saying. "One moment, Mr Field. I'd like a word with ye."

Frances saw the younger man's eyebrows go up and caught his faint smile before he turned and grimaced at her. It was the most reassuring of gestures, revealing a comforting understanding of her mood. She warmed before it gratefully, but as she turned away the new and horrible suspicion came back to her.

"I heard him go out *before* that," she said vehemently to Gabrielle a few moments later as she stood at the end of the bed once more. "It's quite clear in my mind. David went out first that night. I heard the latch click just after I reached the stairhead.

Then about ten minutes later than that someone walked sharply down the passage from the garden room and went out of the front door."

"Yes," said the old Gabrielle placidly. "How deceptive a noise like that is in the night."

They were alone in the enormous bedroom, the two of them, the youngest and the oldest of the Ivorys, and they stood looking at one another, summing each other up for a long time. Years afterwards it occurred to Frances that she grew up at that moment.

She stepped back from the bed and walked over to the fireplace. Her green woollen dress, which had been tailored as only the southern English do tailor, hugged her slim hips and straight shoulders. The old woman among the pillows under the tapestry triptych watched her, an expression that was purely feminine in her eyes.

"I had a nineteen-inch waist when I was twenty-five," she said suddenly, and for the first time in their acquaintance her granddaughter followed her line of thought easily and replied to it without looking round.

"It's my life anyway," she said. "I know what I'm doing. You're wrong about David having designs on my money. He doesn't even want to marry me. The engagement was only a silly stunt to make things easier. I went and bellowed my troubles to him about Lucar. I told you."

Gabrielle glanced at the slim young back. It was a swift stab with the little black eyes, and her husband, Meyrick's father, who had loved her and had needed every one of his shrewd wits to keep up with her, would have recognised the symptom and congratulated his granddaughter.

"You heard the latch click and then afterwards, some time afterwards, you heard someone else cross the hall and go out?"

The question was clear and lucid, with a brain behind it. For the time being Gabrielle had returned from the shadows and inexactitudes of age and her voice was as decisive as ever it had been.

"Yes, I told you. And, Granny, Lucar was in the house that night. I know that because I saw him. I met him when I went down to the garden room."

"When *you* went down to the garden room?"

The interruption was very quiet but it brought the girl swinging round, colour surging over her face, staining her throat and the thin flesh over her temples. She told her story hurriedly.

"I went down to see how David and Robert were getting on together. I met Lucar coming away from the garden room as I went through the hall but I didn't speak to him. He was angry about something and quite insufferable. I went on down the passage, but the door was shut and I didn't like to go barging in so I—I went down into the yard."

"And looked up through the window?" said the old woman unexpectedly. She was sitting up, with her eyes alive as a monkey's, every resource of her frail body roused to meet the exertion of keeping her mind going. "Very sensible. Just what I should have done myself. What did you see?"

Frances regarded her steadily. "Oh, they were just talking, you know," she said deliberately.

"You saw them both?"

"Yes, I did."

"Are you in love?"

"No, I don't think so. I don't know."

Gabrielle lay back. Her face was peaceful and she was half smiling. Frances was half afraid that the excitement had proved too much for her for she was silent for a long time, but when she spoke again it was evident that she was still thinking.

"They say it's unlucky to marry for love," she remarked. "Someone said that. It's not a *bon mot*. Some country saying, I think. Very true. Did you see Field again that night?"

"Yes. He came up to my room to say that we were still engaged and that Robert was going for a walk."

"To your bedroom?"

"Yes, darling."

The old Gabrielle stirred her tiny shoulders, and her mouth, which could ever be cruel, twisted into a *moue* of distaste.

"Quite like a servant girl," she said.

Frances regarded her sombrely and finally shrugged her own shoulders. It was a little skirmish across a century. The fire stirred and a handful of grey ash fell into the grate. The room was quiet for the door was padded with quilted leather, but even in that sanctuary the unusual bustle below stairs was apparent, forcing them to face the situation, impressing them with its breathless urgency.

"We must cable Meyrick." Frances spoke mainly to herself. "That's the first thing to be done."

"We must see the police," snapped Mrs Ivory. "We must find out what they know about it. That's the vital thing. If they want to come up here I'll see them, but you remind them I'm a very old woman."

The final instruction seemed to amuse her and Frances, glancing at her, wondered how much she comprehended of the horror, of the sick feeling of catastrophe, as she peered down upon the scene through the long telescope of her great age.

"What happened to Phillida?" she enquired.

Gabrielle regarded her blankly and once again the girl felt the ground unsteady beneath her feet as she recognised the uncertainty of that fine but fading mind.

"I left her here with Dorothea, darling," she said gently. "Don't you remember?"

As she waited for the reply a clatter of voices beneath the window rose up into the room, and the nightmare quality of her own position swept over her. Gabrielle was a terrifying ally.

"Did you? Perhaps you did." The old woman was not thinking of her words. "I must have got rid of her. I think I did. I told Dorothea to send for a doctor. Phillida's a poor thing. These piteous women without stamina! Fetch me my hand mirror, will you, dear? What's going on out there?"

The final demand was vigorous enough, and Frances threw up the window sash. She looked down at the narrow path which ran round from the front of the house to the yard at the back under an archway between 38 and the gallery. The window was directly above the service exit, and it was here that the noise originated. Mrs Sanderson, the housekeeper, was standing on the flags, the wind swaddling her solid figure in a jumbled drapery of apron, petticoat and twisted stockings. In her arms lay a weeping figure in whose neat blue-suited elegance Frances had some difficulty in recognising Molly, the junior member of the household staff. Molly was crying noisily with her fashionable hat on the back of her head, her face buried in Mrs Sanderson's bosom. Standing before this inelegant and inexplicable group was a solid young man in the boots of a plain-clothes policeman. He held a suitcase in each hand and was using them to shoo the women back into the house.

"Do it inside," he was saying with the weary cheerfulness of the native Londoner. "Have your cry by the kitchen fire, like Christians. Go along, there's good girls. Take her in, Ma. Take her in, do."

"No. It's not right for her to stay. Not another minute. She's doing the right thing. I don't care who you are. If you're a policeman you show me your warrant."

Mrs Sanderson was using her "tradesmen" voice, refinement wearing thin with exasperation and a touch of genuine fishwife to sharpen the steel.

"Dear heaven!" said Gabrielle from the bed.

The comment implied reproach rather than astonishment, and Frances leant out hastily.

"Anything I can do?" she demanded.

The voice from the clouds had the instantaneous effect of all such interruptions. Mrs Sanderson shut her mouth with ominous resolution and Molly's bellowing ceased abruptly. The plain-clothes man put down his suitcases and pulled off his hat.

"Orders are no one is to leave the house, miss," he said politely.

"Oh. Oh, see. All right. Go in, Mrs Sanderson, will you? And you too, Molly. I don't suppose they'll be long, or you can have your day out tomorrow."

A pink and blubbery face was raised to her from the shelter of Mrs Sanderson's cushionly façade.

"I wasn't going out, miss. I was leaving."

"Shame," muttered Mrs Sanderson.

"Really?" Frances was astounded. All Meyrick's servants were very real personalities in his household, and their comings and goings were of general interest to the entire family, so this casual method of departure was an innovation. However, neither the time nor the place was suitable to a domestic discussion.

"Oh, I see. Well, leave tomorrow," she said awkwardly. "Anyway, go in now. I'll come down."

"I wish you would, miss." There was a world of unspoken promise in the housekeeper's voice and she put her arm round Molly, of whom she had never been particularly fond, with considerably more than maternal tenderness.

Frances shut the window and turned back to the dressing table to take up the mirror. Her mind was preoccupied with the curious little incident, so that she did not see Gabrielle until she leaned across the bed to pass the hand glass to her, and then the sudden change in the old woman's appearance came as a shock. Mrs Ivory was sitting bolt upright, her figure puppetlike in its Shetland wrappings and her face shrunk into a yellow doll's mask. Her eyes were alive. They were bright, like a mouse's eyes, and quite as suspicious.

"What did she say?"

"Nothing. It's only that Molly, the little middle maid, appears to be leaving, and a policeman has just turned her back . . . My dear! Granny! Are you all right? Hadn't you better lie down?"

Gabrielle closed her eyes. Without their comforting intelligence she made a terrifying picture.

"Lie down, darling," Frances said firmly. "Lean on my arm and lie back."

The old woman suffered herself to be settled among her cushions.

"It's all very tiring," she said at last with a peevishness which was yet reassuring because of its strength. "Where's Dorothea?"

"I'll get her."

"No. No, don't." A small hand closed over her wrist with surprising force. "Don't. Stay here." She lay still, gripping the girl's arm. Her face was quite calm, and there was no indication that she was in any pain. Presently it occurred to Frances that the grip

was a restraining one rather than any actual need
for support.

"I ought to go down," she said gently. "I'll find
Dorothea for you."

"No." Gabrielle still had her eyes closed. "Frances,
have you ever thought that stepsister of yours was
. . . a little *funny?*"

It was impossible to mistake her meaning, and the
enquiry put so directly and echoing Phillida's own
question about Robert caught Frances off her guard.

"No," she said. "No, darling, of course not."

"You jumped, my dear." The black eyes were open
again and watching her. "Does she talk to you?"

"No, not very much. She's all right. This has been
a terrible shock to her, of course."

"Naturally." Gabrielle spoke primly and was
silent, her lips smiling. "You remind me of your
grandfather," she remarked after a long pause. "He
could never confide. That mania of Phillida's for
doctors, that's unhealthy. She never told you she
heard anything, then?"

"Heard anything?" Even from her mouth the
words had a sinister sound, and she glanced at the
small figure in the bed with misgiving. "When,
darling? On the night Robert was . . . on the night
Robert must have died?"

"Oh no, before. Long before."

"Darling, what are you talking about?" In spite of
herself a rising note crept into the question and
Gabrielle's eyes opened.

"Forget it, my dear," she said placidly. "I'm so

old I imagine things. Listen, there's someone coming across the landing."

Frances turned her head. The house seemed silent for once that morning, holding its breath perhaps.

"I don't think so."

"Yes, there is. My dear child, I haven't slept in this room for thirty years of my life without getting to know it. Open the door."

Frances crossed the room in a wave of loneliness. Robert dead, Meyrick away, the police in the house, Phillida collapsing, David Field—well, David Field very much involved, and now Gabrielle growing fanciful in her senility. The nightmare was becoming ludicrous in its mounting horror. The heavy quilted door slid open noiselessly under her hand and Miss Dorset, who had been hesitating on the threshold, jumped guiltily.

"I didn't like to knock in case she was asleep," she whispered, dragging the startled girl out into the hallway. "I've cabled our branch office at Hong Kong. They'll reach your father, wherever he is. How did it happen? Do you know?"

Everything was painfully vivid that day, and Frances saw a complete picture of the woman vignetted in the archway of the landing. In it every detail was extraordinarily clear, and she saw that her sandy grey hair was poor in its very neatness, while her face was unnaturally sharp, the skin mottled and the five wrinkles across her forehead exaggerated. The unusual excitement had tinged her cheekbones, and there was a forced heartiness about her which undermined her efficiency and made her seem a less reliable person.

"I'm keeping it from the staff at 39 as long as I can," she hurried on. "There 'll be reporters, you know. What would you like done with them?"

Even at that time, when the publicity side of the disaster was a menace unsuspected by most of them, the question struck Frances as absurd.

"What does one do with reporters?" she said and felt cheap as the other woman blushed.

"I can try to send them away," said Miss Dorset defensively, "but sometimes it's as well to issue some sort of statement. There's no one at the gallery who can decide anything. I suppose I'm in command. I can't even get hold of Lucar. He hasn't turned up yet."

"It's late, isn't it?" Frances was vague. Time had become an unconsidered element and years to have passed during the morning.

"Nearly half-past twelve. I phoned his house but he left there at nine. I don't know where he is." Miss Dorset's voice was querulous. "In a way it's better without him, of course, but he ought to know what has happened. Somebody ought to know. I'm coming to the end of my tether, Miss Ivory. I can carry on as long as I've got somebody in authority over me but I'm not used to being alone and . . . "

She paused and the suspicious brightness in her pale eyes brought Frances to her senses.

"Of course you're not, Miss Dorset," she said, laying a hand on the thin arm. "Of course you're not. It's all very dreadful and sudden, but don't worry. We'll get by. You go back and carry on as usual. If you get enquiries about Robert pass them on to me and I'll deal with them. Get hold of Lucar as soon as you can, of course. The police will want to see him."

She paused. The other woman was looking at her eagerly, half fear and half excitement in her expression.

"Then it *was*, was it? I heard something, but I didn't like to ask any more. Who?"

"We don't know. They're finding out now." It was a ridiculous conversation. Evasion of the actual word was instinctive in them both. Miss Dorset's hand shook in the pocket of her coat and her mouth trembled.

"It's dreadful," she said. "In over a hundred years we've never had a breath of scandal and now it's come when your father is away. Are you sure Mr Robert couldn't have done it himself?"

"Well, no. You see, he was found in the cupboard. He must have been hidden there by someone."

Miss Dorset nodded and was silent for a while.

"It's extraordinary," she said at last. "I've often wondered how I should behave if ever I was confronted by a . . . a dreadful crime like this, but now that I am it's just like any other terrible thing, isn't it? I mean it becomes a practical problem. Miss Ivory, I shan't say this to anyone else, but Mr Lucar was over here that night. Did you know?"

"Yes, I saw him."

"Oh." The pale eyes rested on the girl for a moment, but she did not pursue the train of thought. Instead she sniffed and said abruptly: "If it had been the other way round I could understand it. Or if he'd done it himself."

"Could you? Robert was nervy but not suicidal."

"Don't you think so?"

They were still speaking in whispers, and the elder woman's question was sibilant in its sharpness. Frances gaped at her.

"What do you mean? What makes you say that?"

Miss Dorset hesitated, but when her words did come they were so extraordinary that for the second time that day Frances received the sharp little stab in her diaphragm which comes from a fear which is not to be explained, the secret superstitious terror of the utterly unreasonable.

"Did he never talk to you about the whistle on the telephone?" said Miss Dorset. "He didn't?" she added hastily as she saw the girl's expression. "Oh well, then, don't mention it, for heaven's sake. It was probably nothing at all. I ought not to have said anything. I'm so upset today I don't know what I'm doing. I'll go back. I daren't leave the gallery any longer. I'm so glad you're here. You remind me of your father. Did you know you were like him? Any time I'm needed just send over. I shall be there."

Frances caught the angular shoulder just as she was turning away.

"You sound as if you thought Robert was insane."

Miss Dorset eyed her. "I did wonder," she said.

"So would you have done if you'd known him as well as I did."

Frances watched her striding off down the landing in her flat-heeled shoes, a shaken, bewildered, but definitely gallant old maid.

6

THE YOUNGEST IVORY HESITATED. GABRI-
elle's room was quiet and she seized the opportunity
to be alone. She felt a desperate need for a pause, a
minute or two in which to pull herself together and
sort out the facts from this welter of suggestion and
little mysteries which threatened to engulf her.

She turned into her own room mechanically and
entered its cool fastness with a feeling of relief which
was shattered at once as a tall thin figure stepped
back from the window and came towards her.

"Hallo, Duchess," said David Field. "I thought
you must come along here sooner or later. How are
the nerves?"

He stood looking down at her, a cigarette case held
out invitingly, and Frances, who was in that particular state of mind in which the eye sees all things
afresh, found herself thinking that he was a devastatingly good-looking person and that in a way it
was a pity, since so many people must have thought
so before. It was only a momentary respite, however.
In a moment she was back in the crisis again.

"What did they ask you?" she demanded, taking
a cigarette. "Robert was murdered, was he?"

"Looks like it, ducky." She caught his expression

as he held the match for her and was surprised by the impersonal quality of its concern. There was no fear there. He was thinking entirely of her. "The head nark is a nice old Scot," he went on lightly. "You needn't be afraid of him. He's probably even honest. He talked to me like a father. I found myself yearning to confide my secret inhibitions. What's up? Why the wide-open-eye effect?"

Frances, who had not been aware of her change of expression, found the sudden demand confusing.

"There isn't one," she said hastily, and he laughed and put an arm round her shoulders. There was no undue affection in the caress. It was as careless and friendly as his voice.

"You think I'm a mug, don't you?" he said. "You're a most refreshing person, so trusting. I wish I were. Let me tell you, young woman, I'm more experienced than I care to think. Which reminds me, do you recollect performing a Girl Scout act of mercy on my hand with a bottle of iodine some time last week?"

Frances glanced up at him and her eyes flickered. She did remember the incident. He had called in one morning to discuss the announcement of their engagement, amusing her by his secret embarrassment. While they were talking she had noticed a loose flap of skin on his knuckle and had insisted on the antiseptic. She remembered standing in the breakfast room, smearing the stuff on while she told him of Robert's flight to his club. It must have been on the first day, then, on the morning after Robert's death.

"Yes," she said cautiously. "Why?"

He held out his right hand palm downward for her inspection.

"A complete cure," he said. "Gone without trace. Ever heard of Coriolanus?"

"Who?"

"Coriolanus. A hellishly noble Roman. He was touchy about displaying his wounds. I'm just like him. I thought I'd mention it. Forget the incident entirely, will you?"

His arm tightened about her and she stared at him, the full significance of the request breaking over her in a shivery wave which caught her breath and sent the blood flying out of her face. She was looking up at him, her face so near his own that she only saw his mouth. She saw it narrow and twist like a dis-appointed child's, and then he had released her abruptly, flinging her lightly away from him, and was standing before her, laughing.

"Oh, tell 'em what you like, ducky," he said, "but for God's sake don't dramatise the old man."

The reproof was almost spiteful, and she reacted to it instantly.

"I'm not." The retort sounded childish and ridicu-lous in the gravity of the situation. "I'm not. But . . ."

"But what? But what, old water-colour eyes?"

They stood looking at one another, the man de-fensive and ostensibly amused, and the girl hurt and in her heart most desperately afraid.

It was unfortunate that the knock should have

come at that moment or that, as neither of them answered it, the door should have been thrust open by a startled policeman. There was quite a little group on the landing. Norris and a plain-clothes man were there, as well as the elderly Orkney Scot with the hooded grey eyes and the prim expression. Before that owlish and official stare Frances slowly reddened. Beneath his unresponsive glance the room with its muslin curtains, draped dressing table and flounced colonial bed became distressingly feminine and intimate. She glanced at David out of the corner of her eye and saw him grave and slightly at a disadvantage.

"'To the pure all things are slightly indecent,'" he quoted to her under his breath and turned to smile at the elder man. "Have you met Miss Frances Ivory, Inspector?" he enquired. "Frances, this is Mr Bridie, the divisional detective inspector."

"I'm cholly pleased to meet you, Miss Ivory," said the D.D.I., and again the deep Scot's voice with the soft aspirated accent came with a shock of surprise to her. "I'd like a word with ye," he continued and added, looking round him, "We'd hardly talk in he-ere."

There was nothing impolite in his objection; it was simply a statement of his personality, and Frances, who was a stranger to the prurience of the police, felt out of her depth and unjustly ashamed. They all went out on the landing, and Norris and the two subordinate policemen withdrew discreetly to the head of the stairs. Bridie glanced at David.

"I'd like my word wi' the young lady alone," he said mildly.

Frances found herself pouncing on the words, trying to discern any hostility or reassurance in the tone in which they were made, but there was nothing there beyond a polite intimation.

David nodded and drifted off to join the others. He did not touch her, and she found she had expected a reassuring grip on her elbow as he passed and that she experienced an indescribable sense of loss when it did not come.

Bridie led her into the corner of the landing.

"I don't want a statement from ye yet, Miss Ivory," he said. "This is a se-erious business. A bad, nasty business, an' the sooner we get to the bottom of it the better for all concer-rned. I hear your sister's ill and can't be distur-rbed, so the doctor says?" He paused enquiringly.

"My stepsister," said Frances mechanically and wished she had not spoken as his round eyes peered shrewdly at her.

"Your stepsister." He corrected himself. "Ma mistake. I'm sorry." She saw him making a mental note of a lack of sympathy between herself and Phillida as clearly as if he had written it down under her eyes, and her feeling of unsafety grew. "I know who ye are an' all about ye," he went on in a gentle, avuncular fashion as if he were speaking to a child, "an' after a bit I'll ask ye one or two questions, mebbe, but chust now I wondered if perhaps ye'd tek me in to see your granny?"

"To see Gabrielle?" She glanced at the big leather-covered door across the hall.

He nodded. "I've hear-rd she's a pretty old lady and I thought mebbe she'd be more comfortable if ye came with me," he said. "I wouldn't keep her a minute."

"I'll see," she said and hesitated. "Inspector Bridie, what exactly has happened? Was Robert murdered?"

He looked down at her, and his face, with its fine lines and arched eye sockets, was gently disapproving.

"That's a very unpleasant wor-rd, Miss Ivory. Your poor brother-in-law was killed. How it happened I'm attempting to deter-mine."

His ladylikeness provided the finishing touch to the nightmare quality of the situation, and she saw him then for the first time in the light in which she was to see him ever after, as the embodied spirit of that gentle but inexorable and humourless enquiry which is the finest tradition of British police detection.

"I'll see Granny," she said hastily.

Old Mrs Ivory laid down her hand mirror and settled her shawls more carefully about her when Frances brought the divisional detective inspector in some few minutes later. Dorothea stood wooden and disapproving by the head of the imposing bed and Bridie advanced cautiously. He was a little out of his depth in this majestic presence, Frances was grateful to see, and in any other circumstances she might have been sorry for him. The old Gabrielle regarded him steadily. Her back was held stiffly against the pillows and her eyes were alive and imperious.

"I have lived a very long time," she said. Either as a greeting or as an opening gambit the announcement was unexpected and unanswerable and the Scot bowed.

"Ye have indeed, ma'am," he said awkwardly. "I wouldn't venture to intrude upon ye if the circumstances didn't make it ver-ry desir-rable."

The old lady listened to him with evident pleasure, for she smiled.

"What is Scotland like nowadays?" she enquired. "I used to go up to Braemar in the season, long ago. Those poor deer, Frances. So pathetic. Velvet faces and tiny feet, like women in tight shoes."

Bridie shot an imploring glance at the girl, who went forward.

"Darling, this is the divisional detective inspector. He wants to talk to you about Robert."

"Robert," said Gabrielle, and a shadow passed over her face. "Oh yes, of course, of course, I was forgetting. I forget so much. So you're a policeman?"

The final question was put sharply and Bridie stiffened.

"I am, ma'am."

"The police," said Gabrielle and sighed, "in our house. I remember. I remember. Of course. Poor Robert died yesterday."

"Yesterday?" It seemed to Frances that he pounced upon the word as if it had been an admission.

"Yes," said Gabrielle, "and they only told me this morning. You told me, Dorothea." She turned to the servant with a tiny fluttering gesture which brought back the ghosts of the drawing rooms of the eighties.

"I did, my dearie, I did." Old Dorothea patted the tiny outstretched hand and glowered at the inspector with a wealth of unspoken indignation. He looked uncomfortable but stood his ground.

"It's part of my cheneral duties to enquire if there was anyone who had taken any especial dislike to him, ma'am," he said.

Gabrielle closed her eyes.

"Robert," she said. "Poor Robert. I never liked him myself. I remember him quite well. He and my husband were not friends but business associates. They never quarrelled but they were never intimate."

"Darling, you mean Meyrick, don't you? Meyrick, my father. Your son, not your husband." Frances made the interruption quickly. The fires had died down again. The vital Gabrielle of the morning had disappeared into the shadows once more. This was a very old woman rambling up and down among her memories like a child in a garden.

"Meyrick?" The bright black eyes flicked open with interest. "Where is Meyrick? Send Meyrick up here now at once. I've been asking and waiting for Meyrick for hours. Why isn't he here? Business must wait. I can't deal with people at my age. He must know that I can't look after him all his life."

Dorothea bent over the bed.

"He's away, ma'am. He's abroad, my dear. I keep

telling you. You're tired, my lady. You lie down.
Mr Meyrick will come sooner or later. Don't you
keep fretting."

Her tone was intentionally soothing, but underlying it resentment seethed and boiled. Gabrielle
seemed to notice it for she laughed softly.

"Poor Phyllis," she said. "No, it's not Phyllis,
is it? I had Phyllis when Meyrick was born. Poor
Dorothea and poor Gabrielle. Poor Gabrielle is old.
Old. Too old. Let me think. Ask your question
again, my man."

It was a gallant effort; the old mind struggling to
continue to rouse itself into working order was
pathetic, and Bridie's troubled expression grew.

"Ye were saying that ye weren't ver-ry fond of
Mr Robert Madrigal yourself, ma'am," he said.
"Ye had a few wor-rds wi' him when ye came up
here from Hampstead, mebbe?"

"No." Gabrielle seemed perfectly lucid and even
forceful. "He was rude to me and I told him I should
stay here in my own room until Meyrick returned."

"Until your son retur-rned," said Bridie, snapping
down upon what he appeared to regard as an admission.

"Certainly," agreed Gabrielle. "Until my son
returned from business."

"Or from abroad?"

The old Gabrielle looked a little frightened. Her
black eyes flickered and she moved her hands helplessly. Finally she began to laugh. It was no sound of
mere amusement, but the studied social laugh of the

very old actress, the laugh to cover the faux pas or the awkward pause.

"I forget," she said to Bridie with all the gracious apology of her period and her breeding and all the charm of her eternal femininity. "I'm so old. I forget. Forgive me."

He looked embarrassed, as well he might have been, and Dorothea with her eyes watering bent over her mistress again.

"It's death," she whispered. "Mr Madrigal is dead, ma'am. They've found Miss Phillida's husband dead in the cupboard downstairs. I told you."

Gabrielle stared at her with the astonished look of the baby or the wandering mind.

"Was that today?" she said. "I thought my husband was with me when you came in to tell me that. He *was* here. He went downstairs to see him. Oh, dear, the years close up on me. I've no sense of time, none at all, none at all. I thought that was years ago. Robert Madrigal dead today and the police in the house? Oh, dear."

Her voice died away, but her thin lips continued to mumble and her black eyes were troubled and helpless.

Bridie's attitude underwent a complete change.

"I'll apologise for intruding on ye, ma'am," he said, and evidently Gabrielle's old charm had not deserted her for he looked as gallant and as virile as an old man with a prim face and a sober suit may well be. "I won't trouble ye any longer." He raised his voice a little as if he were speaking to old and

deaf royalty. "I'll thank ye ver-ry much and I'll
ask ye to excuse me. Good mor-rning."

"Good morning," said Gabrielle and remarked to
Dorothea before he was out of the room, "a nice
creature. Who did you say he was?"

The divisional detective inspector looked younger
and his colour had heightened when he came out onto
the deserted landing again.

"She's a grand old lady," he said to Frances in a
burst of confidence which he did not often permit
himself, "but remar-rkably old. I hear-rd she was
almost ninety but I hadn't enveesaged it, if you take
my meaning. I'm cholly grateful to you for taking
me in. I'm glad I saw her. When one's old like that
the days and the year-rs appear to get mixed up in
one's mind." He sighed and added seriously: "What
an awful thing for a poor old body like that! She
came here over a week ago, you say?"

"Yes. On the day Robert—on the day we thought
Robert went away."

"Ah, she did?" He reconfirmed the point. "That's
chust what I under-rstood. And she was thinking
about her son, your father, about that time, wasn't
she?"

"Yes, I suppose she was. I'd been talking to her
about him that afternoon."

"Ye had?" He seemed pleased. "Mebbe that
accounts for it. I could not make up ma mind until
I'd seen her, only ye see, on the mor-rning after she
came here, ear-rly, before the news of Mr Madrigal's
so-called departure was announced, she sent the

wee maid Molly down to the post office wi' a cable
to your father's agents in Hong Kong. The girl can't
remember the message wor-rd for wor-rd, but it was
for him to come home immediately. Did ye know
that?"

Her face answered him, and he laughed at her
kindly.

"Ye'd never mek a liar-r," he said and added,
relapsing into his habitual gravity, "it's a cholly
unpleasant business for ye all but chustice must be
ser-rved."

He was silent for some little time and then startled
her out of her senses by a second question.

"Did you know the little maid, Molly, was dismissed this mor-rning by the old woman who waits
on your granny? Tur-rned out of the hoose, she
was, not a quar-rter of an hoor after the body was
found."

7

FRANCES WAS ALONE IN THE BREAKFAST
room early the following morning. She sat before an
untouched tray, staring moodily out through the
fine net curtains at the grey late autumn day tinged
with that faint melancholy yellow which is peculiar
to London when Miss Dorset came running over with
the news. She still wore her hat and coat, and there
were rime beads on the sandy grey curl of hair on
her forehead. She came in breathlessly, shut the door
behind her with unconsciously exaggerated caution
and advanced to the table, leaning upon it with one
capable hand.

"He's gone," she said.

"Who? Lucar?"

It may have been an ungenerous reaction, but
Frances felt her heart jolt with pure hopefulness.

Miss Dorset nodded. Her eyes were bright and her
shiny face glowed with excitement.

"Can you beat it? It went through my head yesterday, but I didn't like to say anything of course. I got
on to his flat as early as I dared this morning, and his
servant said he's still not back. He walked out just
before nine yesterday morning and he hasn't been

seen since. There's only one explanation that comes to one's mind, isn't there?"

Frances got up. "My God," she said involuntarily. "If it's true. If only it's true!"

Miss Dorset looked at her curiously. "I felt like that myself," she said and sniffed. "It's a relief. There 'll be a trial when they catch him, you know. That 'll be bad enough, with us all in the witness box. The police are after him already. The servant told me there's been a man hanging about the place all night. Well, I'm not surprised. I never liked Lucar and I never trusted him further than I could see him. He was behind all that trouble we've been having at the gallery. I've known that from the beginning. Naturally I couldn't do or say anything about it with Robert Madrigal in charge. *He* had me frightened out of my wits at the end of the time. Poor man, you can't help being sorry for him. It doesn't seem possible, does it? How *was* he killed? Do you know?"

"No, I don't." The girl's face was haggard and the delicate line of her chin fine-drawn. "I don't, Miss Dorset. That's the most terrifying part of the whole thing. None of us knows anything. The entire affair has been taken out of our hands. We're not even in it. The police come and go and hang round the house and send for us and ask questions and go away again. Norris seems to know most and he gets that by gossiping with the detective on the back entrance. I feel as though we were all sitting blindfolded in a glass case. Everyone can see us and we can't see anybody, not even each other."

Miss Dorset sat down heavily.

"It is a bit like that," she agreed. "Old Mr Worthington wasn't too helpful, was he? Still, you can't expect an elderly solicitor of that sort to be at his best in a case like this. He's never had anything more serious from us than a breach of contract in his life. I sent him round, though, you see, because you must all be represented at the inquest, and he was Mr Madrigal's man as well as the firm's."

"He was very kind," said Frances dubiously. "He was here all yesterday afternoon. Phillida couldn't see him, but Gabrielle kept him talking for hours. I tried to get a little information out of him, but he simply patted my hand and told me not to worry. I may be wrong, but my impression was that he didn't want to be mixed up in anything unpleasant."

Miss Dorset raised her pale eyes.

"You can't really blame him, can you?" she said bluntly, and the words were so unexpected that Frances showed her surprise and she laughed awkwardly. "It's not so bad now we know it was Lucar," she said in a singularly unfortunate attempt to sound comforting. "Before that, well, it was very awkward, wasn't it? I mean, my dear, it was so obviously someone in the house that night."

There is nothing more brutal than the plain truth kindly meant, and Frances felt the ground tremble beneath her feet.

"I suppose it was," she said dully.

"Well, naturally." Miss Dorset laughed the dry little laugh of the common sensed. "That's the shock-

ing thing about these really dreadful affairs. They
always are just about as bad as they look at first
sight. I was very frightened for you yesterday. . . .
He's such a nice man, isn't he? I've admired his
painting for years."

There was no mistaking her inference, and the thin
blush on her cheeks drove the observation home.

"Oh, I never thought that David had anything to
do with it," began Frances firmly, hoping that her
face would not betray her.

Miss Dorset squeezed her arm.

"Of course you didn't, my dear," she said devastatingly. "No one would have expected you to."

There was a difficult pause and she went on
hurriedly.

"I haven't had a reply to my China cable yet.
Your father really is needed here. There's no one in
authority left at all next door, except me."

Frances was contrite. "Daddy's coming. I forgot
to tell you. A message came last night after you'd
gone home. This fantastic news about Lucar put
everything else out of my mind. He wired from
Alexandria. He's coming on by plane this morning.
He'll be here tomorrow. Apparently Gabrielle cabled
him last week."

"She did?" Miss Dorset was astounded. For an
instant her pale blue eyes were suspicious, and at that
danger signal Frances recovered the new poise and
caution which had momentarily deserted her.

"Yes," she said easily, turning from the window,
her long thin hands clasped idly behind her. "It must

BLACK PLUMES
=======

74

have been my fault. Last week I got windy over the
conditions at the gallery and I went up to Hampstead
with a tale of woe, and apparently I frightened the
old darling and she went into action and sent for
Papa."

The story sounded convincing, and if it were not
the truth at least it would have to serve. Miss Dorset
was appeased.

"Tomorrow," she said, and had she been a younger
and more personable woman the heartfelt satisfaction
in her voice might have been misunderstood. "That
is good news. Oh, I am glad. Oh well, then, we shall
all be perfectly all right. I'll look up the plane and
send the car down to meet him. Tomorrow? Really
tomorrow? I hadn't hoped for anything as soon as
that. I can't tell you how that has cheered me up.
There's a lot of news for him. Mr Godolphin, for one
thing. I was glad to hear that he was safe after all
this time, but I've not had a moment to think of him.
Your father will be delighted over that. Oh dear,
this is good!"

Her smile was transfiguring.

"It's a terrible home-coming, of course," she added
with sudden gravity. "Poor man, what a shock! Still,
I shall be relieved to see him."

She was frankly dithering, and her very unself-
consciousness was evidence of that modern relation-
ship which is the affection of the ideal feminine
lieutenant for her employer, than which there is no
more unselfish service.

This information appeared to have quite superseded her own news of importance and she went off almost immediately, completely preoccupied with preparations for Meyrick's return. Robert Madrigal might have been murdered and Lucar might be hounded for the crime, but for Miss Dorset the principal excitement of the moment was the blessed home-coming of the boss.

The youngest Ivory remained by the window, the straggling yellow light spilling on her hair and her unexpectedly firm chin. Long afterwards, when she looked back on that early morning, it seemed to her that the two hours of comparative peace which followed it were the lull before the hurricane and a special dispensation of providence to enable her to get her breath before the buffeting whirlwind of catastrophe which was to come.

Gabrielle was still asleep in her great brass bed, with Matthew, Mark, Luke and John blessing her in gros point. Phillida was too prostrate to be disturbed, and then there seemed no sense in breaking in on either of them with the gossip.

So it had been Lucar. The information lifted a weight off her lungs as surely as if it had been a physical reality. She felt she could breathe and think again.

She began to think at once of David and she saw him again in her mind's eye as she had seen him from the yard that night when the wind had danced and frolicked about her like a live and malignant thing. He was quite clear in her memory, standing in the garden room looking down at something with no expression at all on his face. Looking *down* . . . And then the idiotic request for secrecy about his injured hand.

She walked down the room to rid herself of this line of reasoning and came to a full stop, wondering again exactly how Robert had been killed. It would make it all so much easier if she knew the details. She wrenched her mind away with a deliberate effort, and forced herself to think of Lucar. Apart from the fact that he was the sort of man whom one would hope to find guilty of any serious crime in his vicinity, he had practically proved it by running away. Yet it was not going to be quite so easy, she realised, with a return of her old heaviness. Her memory was honest and relentless. Whole scenes returned to her as vividly as if she were seeing them on a cinema screen. When she had met Lucar at the end of the garden-room passage he had been speechless with injured pride, disappointment and jealousy. Those had been the emotions which had controlled him. They had been clear in his face and in every line of his short-legged, undistinguished body. He had looked at the ring on her hand and had flung himself out of the house. Conceivably he might have come creeping back afterwards, but if so no one had seen or heard him, and the front door had a spring lock.

Meanwhile David had certainly been in the garden room after Lucar had left. She herself had seen him there, looking down . . .

It was odd that not until then did she remember the handle of the shed turning so slowly in the shaft

of light. Until now she had dismissed it as evidence
of her own unbalanced imagination, but now in the
daylight, with the new evidence which the past
twenty-four hours had revealed, the picture came
back to her with fresh certainty. Someone must have
been in that shed. Someone must have stood hidden
in that fitful, breathy darkness, watching and waiting. It could not have been Lucar. She had heard
the front door clang behind him as she went down
the passage and, even had he rushed round to the
back of the house immediately, she must have seen
him as she came out onto the iron staircase.

Nor could it have been David, for David had been
in the garden room, framed in the brilliant square of
the lighted window, even while she watched the
handle turn.

Who was it, then? Who else had been moving about
the quiet shadowy house that night?

Finally she obeyed her impulse to go down to the
yard and look at the shed by daylight. Without
pausing to consider why, she avoided the garden-
room passage and went out through the kitchen,
where an unnatural gloom prevailed. She received
a pitying leer from Mrs Sanderson, which made her
feel like some particularly ludicrous orphan in a
pantomime storm, while Molly, though reinstated
at Frances' own instigation, glowered at her unreasonably from above a pile of potato peelings.
Mercifully neither of them was inclined to talk,
and she came out into the yard to see it with the new
eyes which disaster lends to familiar objects as a

shabbier, homelier place than it had appeared a week
before on that night when the wind had been high
and the shadows had made mountains of the tall
houses on its border.

Today, when the weather was muggy with a
promise of fog and a half promise of fog behind that,
the erstwhile rose garden looked small and dirty, as
such air shafts do in a small city.

Frances went over to the shed feeling foolishly
guilty. She had no idea what she expected to find in
it. Whoever had been hiding there a week before
would not, presumably, be there still. Nevertheless
she turned the handle cautiously and with some of
the wild panic of childhood drew the door open.

She had moved slowly but not quite slowly enough.
Although the small room was in darkness the atmosphere struck warm, and out of the tail of her eye she
caught the fleeting impression of light hastily ex-
tinguished. She stood still, her flesh crawling.

"Who," she began in a small unnatural voice,
"who's there?"

There was no reply, no movement, and she wavered.
The obvious thing to do was to fasten the door and
to go back to the house for a light, and she was
drawing back when the voice came, casual and unexpectedly familiar.

"It's you, is it, Miss Ivory? Chust come in a moment, will you?"

Divisional Detective Inspector Bridie switched on
his torch as he spoke, and the dusty cavern shot into
view. He was sitting on an upturned packing case

in the far corner, using a pile of whitewood boards as a temporary table. Frances gaped at him.

"You frightened me," she said, speaking directly because it was the truth. "What on earth are you doing here in the dark?"

He chuckled. "Minding my own business," he said affably, adding, since it was his custom to give an adequate reason for everything he did so that nothing was to be lost by it, "I tur-rned off my light to see what ye might be going to do doon here. Why did you come snooping ar-round?"

"I didn't."

He shrugged his shoulders.

"That's a cholly silly thing to say when I saw ye myself." He made the comment carelessly and bent over the ledge in front of him. A great many people besides Frances Ivory had found Ian Alexander Bridie an impossible man with whom to argue. She came further into the shed, struggling with a natural inclination to justify herself, and came to an abrupt pause as she took in the extraordinary collection lying under his square hands. There were some fifteen or twenty long narrow implements, ranging from an ordinary meat skewer to a fine mounting knife in a bone holder, spread out on the whitewood pile.

He let her look for a long time and suddenly swung round, torch in hand, so that the beam fell directly on her face. Evidently what he saw there disappointed him for he set the light down again and sighed.

"I've made a cheneral sear-rch of the two houses,"

he said conversationally. "I've been everywhere except in your granny's bedroom. Ye can't think of any other wee weapon in this sor-rt of shape, can ye?"

Frances took up a long, blunt blade mounted in a petit-point covered handle. It was one of those mysterious and apparently useless gadgets which had come in a box containing a buttonhook and a shoehorn.

"That's mine," she said, her natural indignation mingling uncomfortably with a new feeling of personal insecurity.

"I know it is," he agreed. "I took it out of a drawer in your dresser. It's too big and too blunt, I'm afraid. That's the sort of chigger I'm after, but it's over shor-rt." He indicated the mounting knife as he spoke. "The old man in the workshop swore it was the longest he had seen in the trade, and I doubt me if he was lying."

"Was Robert killed like that?"

He did not answer her and had half convinced her that he had not heard the question when he turned his head unexpectedly and his cold eyes met hers not unkindly.

"If ye'll say why ye were snooping round in here mebbe I'll tell ye," he suggested. "After all, it 'll likely be in the evening papers."

Whether the final observation was a salve to his professional caution or part of his natural bent for a hard bargain was not apparent.

"I came down to see if there was anyone—anything here," she said at last.

"Ye said 'anyone,'" he objected. "A lurkin' blackamoor, mebbe?"

"A what?"

He laughed. "Ye don't listen to ser-rvants' gossip, I see," he said cryptically. "Well, who was it ye were looking for? The wee red-hair-red fellow?"

This time he struck a bull's-eye and seemed pleased at her change of face. Frances stiffened. He was a dangerous old man, an old man who caught one out and surprised one into dangerous admissions.

"I certainly didn't come here to look for Henry Lucar," she said firmly. "Please get that idea out of your mind. Even if I wanted to find him, which isn't really very likely, I should hardly come looking for him in an outhouse. I only thought that if anyone was hanging about the house that night this would have been the one place in which they could have hidden and kept an eye on the garden room."

"Ah." He had turned on his packing case and now sat, regarding her contemplatively. "Ye thought that, did ye? So did I. Well, I'll keep my bargain. The deceased was killed by a chab in the chest, passing between the fourth and fifth ribs and pier-rcing the hear-rt bag. The blade of the weapon was appr-roximately half an inch or two longer." He jerked his head at the collection on the pile of wood behind him. "These are all overshort," he repeated, "but I'll take 'em along. They're the best I can find."

While she was still digesting this gruesome information he leant forward and remarked quietly: "That's very chenerous of me, considering that ye did not think fit to mention that ye came down to the yar-rd here ye'self on the night of the crime."

She stared at him. Her heart had leapt so violently that her first thought was that he must have heard it.

"How do you know?" It was an idiotic question, revealing and acquiescing, and she heard it come out of her mouth with dismay.

"Your granny's old maid told me."

"Dorothea?"

He nodded and she stood looking at him, unaware of the picture she made with her head held up a little and the conflicting lights meeting on the clean youthful lines of her face and throat. Dorothea had told him. Dorothea, who had evidently heard it from Gabrielle. It seemed a peculiar piece of secondhand information for her to pass on unless she had some very good reason for doing so, or unless she had offered it as a sop to Cerberus while she hid something more important.

"What else did she tell you?" she enquired evenly.

"I'd prefer the story from you."

"All right. I did come here that night. I didn't like to interrupt David and Robert by going into the room, so I came out here to see if I could see in through the window. They were talking about my engagement, you see, so naturally I wondered how the interview was going."

"Naturally," he said, and she thought his mouth twisted in a half-smile. "How long would you have stood in the yar-rd?"

"About a minute. Perhaps two."

"No longer?" His surprise was justifiable and she was eager to explain.

"No, I ran in almost at once. I was . . . I mean something frightened me."

"What was that?" He made it sound a most prosaic question, and she told him the story of the shed door opening with growing discomfort.

It did not make a very convincing story, but if Bridie was unimpressed he did not show it. He noted down the facts on the back of an old envelope without comment.

"Now," he said at last, "when ye looked through the window what did ye see?"

"David and Robert talking." She had told this lie before and it came glibly.

Bridie's pencil hovered over the page, and beneath their deep arches his eyes were thoughtful.

"Ye're certain ye saw both men?"

"Yes."

"Chust talking?"

"Yes."

He sighed and replaced the envelope.

"Ah well," he said, "I'll not be keeping ye, Miss Ivory. Thank ye for your help. By the way," he added as she turned towards the door, "there's one wee point I forgot to mention when I was telling ye how the deceased met his death. There was a contusion on the back of the poor chap's heid and another on his chin. The one on his chin was likely made by a blow from a fist an' was delivered with such violence that there's a likelihood that the assailant's hand

was damaged. Now, during this week you've seen
Henry Lucar who's missing. Have ye noticed any
mark on his hand?"

It was such a highly improper question from a
police officer that she saw the trap, and for once
Divisional Detective Inspector Ian Alexander Bridie
was, as he would have said himself, "cholly well too
clever by half, no question about that."

"No," she said so coolly that he was not sure if she
was controlling herself by a superb effort or merely
registering disapproval of his methods of interro-
gation. "I'm afraid I haven't. It's hardly a thing I
should have noticed."

Bridie resigned himself to this defeat philosophi-
cally, as was his temperament.

"Likely not," he agreed and waited slyly until
she was half out of the door before he added briskly,
"he's in the hoose now, ye know. Came in forty
minutes since and went straight up to your sister—
excuse me, half sister."

Frances turned in astonishment.

"Lucar?" she demanded.

"Oh no." He watched her carefully as he spoke.
"He's still away, the deleeriously silly fellow. I was
speaking of your fiancé, Mr Field. Haven't you seen
him this mor-rning? I thought it was odd him coming
and asking directly for Mrs Madrigal and odder
still that she should see him. Ah well, I'll not detain
ye. Ye'll be anxious to get away to him, no doubt.
Never concern yourself about me. I'll chust be in and
out all the day most likely."

8

IT IS QUITE POSSIBLE TO CROSS A YARD,
enter a house and climb up two flights of stairs without being conscious of movement. Had Frances
arrived outside Phillida's door by magic carpet she
could not have been less aware of the journey.
Petrifying terror had taken possession of her. At that
time she had no jealousy. Had that most degrading
of the emotions had any place in her make-up then
she would never have burst in on them so uncere-
moniously. At that moment she was only afraid for
David, afraid for him and of him and of her ignorance
concerning him. She did not even knock but wrenched
open the door and went straight in, coming to an
abrupt halt halfway across the plum-coloured
carpet.

By daylight the room's modern opulence was
faintly offensive. Stripped wood and regency colours
combined to give it a somewhat overpowering elegance. David and Phillida were caught in their pose
like figures on a canvas, vivid against the rich, warm
background. They sat on either side of a narrow
walnut table, with the gilt telephone between them.
Phillida's green house coat was in quilted satin and
its train spread out behind her where the deep pile of

the carpet had caught the silk. Her long bare arms
were stretched out across the wood, her head between
them bowed in an abandonment of misery. David
held her wrists, his hands looking solid and masculine
against the transparency of her skin. He was half
out of his chair, an arrested picture of compassionate
eagerness.

It was only for an instant, of course. Before the
door had closed he was on his feet, his hands in his
pockets and his uncomfortably handsome face grave
and embarrassed, while Phillida sat up slowly and
looked at the newcomer with great drowned, pale
blue eyes. Nobody spoke. There was a full minute
of complete silence, during which Frances realised
firstly that there was some sort of emotional crisis
going on, secondly that they had some secret from
which she was excluded and finally and most shatter-
ingly that there was no earthly reason why these
things should not be. After all, she had no proprietory
claim on David. Their engagement had been an act
of courtesy and obviously did not entail fidelity.

The sensation of disappointment and loneliness
which swept over her was so salutary that it startled
her into her senses and she grew slowly crimson.

"I'm terribly sorry, you two," she began. "Shall I
get out, or . . . "

Her voice died. They were neither of them looking
at her but were both eying the telephone with the
same degree of fascinated interest. As they watched
it began to ring.

Phillida put out her hand and picked up the receiver. She was green. Her mouth was stiff and unmanageable and she closed her eyes.

"Yes?" she said huskily.

Frances stole a glance at David. He was watching the other woman with a grimace of apprehension with which one motorist observes another approaching a dangerous accident.

"Yes?" said Phillida again, the word scarcely articulate. "Yes . . . It's me . . . Phillida. Oh, my dear, don't . . . don't bother . . . What? Oh, I am. I am, I am. . . ." The last word was a cry, and a long pause followed while the instrument crackled excitedly. "When?"

The fear in her voice startled both listeners. Her eyes had opened and were wide and ugly.

"So soon? I see . . . Yes, I'm glad. Of course I'm glad. Of course I am. Of course . . . Good-bye . . . Darling, good-bye. . . ."

The instrument clicked but she did not replace it, but sat staring stupidly in front of her. In the end it was David who took the telephone from her and put it back on its stand.

"You didn't tell him," he said accusingly.

She shook her head and began to cry. He turned away from her and strode down the room, jingling the money in his pockets with a nervous irritable gesture so different from his usual lazy manner that Frances was bewildered.

"You ought to have," he said over his shoulder. "It was the only possible thing to do. When does he get here?"

"On Thursday." Phillida whispered the words as if they had been a pronouncement of doom.

"A day after Meyrick? My God, suppose something happens and they meet on the train and the old man tells him."

"Don't, David, don't. Don't, I can't stand it. I can't, I can't, I can't!"

The last word was drowned in a storm of passionate crying. She flung herself across the table and wept with a complete abandonment which was horrible, and, if it had not been so distressing, ludicrous.

David paused abruptly in his restless wandering and, going over to her, he put his hands under her arms and lifted her up.

"Stop it," he said sharply. "Stop it, Phillida. Stop it, d'you hear? Pull yourself together. Lie down on this couch thing and pull yourself together. It's the only thing to do."

He put her down gently on the day bed and, taking an eiderdown from the foot, threw it over her.

"Sleep," he said. "You'll want to in a minute, after all that. Sleep, and for heaven's sake get a little courage."

It was considered brutality, expedient in the circumstances. Mrs Madrigal's hysteria died away, to give place to quiet weeping. She lay with her face hidden and her hair sprawling over the silk pillows. For a moment the man remained looking down at her. Gradually his own tension relaxed, the careless smile returned to his eyes, and his wide mouth twisted with compassion.

"Poor old girl," he said. "God knows I'm sorry."

She did not move, and presently he turned away towards the door. Frances genuinely thought he was unaware of her own presence altogether. Throughout the whole extraordinary scene, which had lasted scarcely five minutes, he had never once looked in her direction, but now, on his way to the door, he thrust out an arm and collected her, holding her tightly and sweeping her out of the room with him.

"God, what a time to come barging in!" he said as he closed the latch behind them.

The remark was so easy and so friendly and yet so immeasurably more adult than any expression of her own reactions that she was both taken off her guard and comforted.

"I'm sorry," she began diffidently. "I had no idea . . ."

He took his arm from her shoulders and pushed her head gently on to one side with the flat of his hand.

"Come off it, ducky," he said. "For the love of old Uncle George and the Fourteen Exotics come off it. This isn't the time. That was 'Dolly' Godolphin. Just before you made your entrance the telephone people had announced that a personal call from him to Phillida was due at any moment. Hence the tension. God knows where he was ringing from. I forgot to ask the poor girl. Basra, perhaps, since he's due in the day after tomorrow. Let's go out and have a drink. I need it if you don't."

"No, I don't think I will, not at the moment."

"Why not? My good girl, you can't hang about

this ghastly house day in and day out. It's unhealthy.
It 'll get on your nerves. You'll get hysterical. Let's
get out of this, if only for ten minutes. It 'll mean that
the lad from the police station who follows me about
with such doglike devotion has to air his boots again,
but I don't see why we should worry about him."

"Are they following you already?" She spoke
involuntarily and he raised his eyebrows in genuine
astonishment.

"Darling, you're all white and positively tremu-
lous. Isn't that nice? You flatter the old man and
make him feel silly. Go and put your hat on. Remember every second saved in the operation means
another half inch in the vine tendrils growing round
my heart."

He was only half laughing at her and there was a
suggestion of unusual colour on his high cheekbones.
They were standing on the big dim landing together,
surrounded by the closed doors behind which drama,
growing every hour, was gathering force and mo-
mentum. Frances was very much aware of it all, dark
and emotional, mysterious and quite unbearable.

"No," she said definitely. "No, David, I don't
want to."

He put both hands on her shoulders and looked
into her face. Afterwards she could never make up
her mind if his curious half-smile was mischievous,
derisive or as oddly shy as it seemed at the time.

"Marry me this afternoon?" he said and waited
for incredulity to appear in her eyes.

It came and he laughed, letting her go instantly.

"Why?" Frances was still young enough to put the question in spite of the tension of the hour.

He grimaced at her. "The iodine-stained hand," he said. "By the laws of England no wife can give evidence against her husband. You asked for it, sweetheart. Now will you come out to lunch?"

It was in the grillroom of the comfortable old Biarritz, with its geraniums, its Turkey carpet and its blessed atmosphere of sensible bonhomie, that the little incident occurred. David was buttonholed in the foyer by a man who was obviously a stranger to him, and Frances went on into the restaurant alone. Bertram, the headwaiter, who made a fortune by greeting every client as if he had been in the service of his family since boyhood, had found her a table near the Piccadilly windows, and she had just settled herself when she saw a familiar face coming down the room towards her at the head of a procession. It was Margaret Fysher-Sprigge with a covey of her cronies fresh from one of their eternal committee meetings. She raised her head and smiled as one does smile at the acquaintance of a lifetime and caught the full gamut of the changing expressions on the haggard parrot face. She saw the first formal grin, the wave of startled recognition, the deep flush of embarrassment and the quick snap of the mouth and hardening of the eyes as the face set into the stony mask which is impenetrable. Mrs Sprigge passed on.

It was the first time in her life that Frances had been cut and she knew suddenly that it would not be

the last. The polite phone calls which had kept the
entire house busy on the day before had been curiously infrequent this morning since the papers had
come out. She was sitting stiffly at the table, her
ears burning, when David came up. He looked irritated.

"A damned reporter," he said as he sat down. "I
nearly gave him a signed confession and the com-
missionaire's hat. Have they been much of a nuisance
at the house?"

"No. The police see them."

"Oh, of course. God bless the laws of libel and
contempt of court. What's the matter with you?"

She told him and he listened with a faintly apprehensive expression which she had not seen in him
before.

"Where is she?" he said at last, looking round.
"That old trout in the wide awake? Never mind
about her. Think of her in the nude." He grinned at
her and, leaning forward, laid a hand over hers.
"There's nothing like it," he said earnestly. "When
insulted by a fish think of it skinned. It takes the edge
off anything."

He was treating her like a child, she saw, and
she wondered why she did not resent it. It was not
a very pleasant meal nevertheless. They were served
with suspicious alacrity, and Frances, already self-
conscious, thought she noticed a corresponding
embarrassment beneath his determined good humour.
He did not refer to Phillida, and Frances found that
she did not want to broach that particular subject,

although it was certainly one which needed an explanation.

At last, as the coffee arrived hard on the dessert, and a couple of apologetic waiters hovered anxiously waiting for them to finish it, he pushed a cigarette case towards her and eyed her under his lashes.

"'Dolly' home on Thursday," he said softly. "There are storms ahead, Duchess. Button down your sou'wester and keep your chin in."

"What do you mean?"

He leant back in his chair and regarded her uncomfortably. He was still smiling superficially, but his round eyes were serious and compassionate. He sighed and shrugged his shoulders.

"Damn all the trouts," he said unexpectedly. "Where were you when 'Dolly' was around before?"

"In Switzerland most of the time, finishing my education. I met him of course."

"Of course," he agreed absently. "You won't have forgotten him. A colourful bird. I never met a chap with more life or more romance about him. This sensational return from death is typical. The story itself was so terrific, and this cap to it supplies just the right touch of the supernatural to make it like him."

They were both silent for a while, remembering the story of Godolphin's death which had moved the world. It had been the Scott incident over again. The three white men with a handful of natives had been forced back by impossible conditions when they were in sighting distance of their goal, the avalanche-

ruined lamasery of Tang Quing, perched precariously
on the side of a peak which had been rendered well-
nigh unclimbable by the disaster. It had been a
perilous retreat. Robert was already ill and the
natives were frightened and refractory. The crowning
tragedy had come when Godolphin smashed his shin-
bone while negotiating a particularly awkward drop.
For two days they had struggled on, carrying him
between them down the narrow, broken track. On
the third night they had camped on the edge of a
snow field, and in the darkness Godolphin had disappeared. There was nowhere for him to have gone
save out into some snow-filled crevasse, and it was
a miracle how he could have dragged himself even so
far. The natives lost their heads in superstitious
terror, and finally the two remaining white men, their
shouts unanswered, realised that exploration was
suicidal and had been forced to accept his gesture
and to struggle on alone.

David shook his head.

"Astounding," he said. "A miracle, and so like
him. Things are not so hot, lady. Not at all so hot."

Frances sat up. The meal and the change of atmosphere had restored her perspective, and she was
exasperated by him.

"Never mind about Godolphin," she said vehemently. "Surely that's the least of the problems!
You've let Phillida work you into a flap about a silly
sentimental situation which might be tragic and
exciting in ordinary circumstances, but now it's
purely idiotic. Don't be insane. Don't be blind. I

know Phillida wasn't in love with Robert, which is
a mercy, but even she doesn't seem to realise that
somebody's killed him and that Lucar has run away,
but . . . but the police don't seem to be as interested
in him as they ought to be."

She broke off, looking at him, her eyes shining with
helpless anxiety.

"Can't you see, you silly romantic ape, they're
interested in you?"

He sat very still, staring at her with no expression
on his face at all, and it came back to her with a sudden stab that this was how he looked when she had
seen him from the yard . . . no expression at all and
looking down.

When he did speak he made the last remark she
could have expected. It was penetratingly true and
quite unpardonable.

"Jealous, ducky?" he enquired.

Frances got up. Afterwards, when she had forgotten the intolerable nervous strain of the preceding
twenty-four hours, she wondered at her lack of
control.

David caught up with her as she crossed the road
to turn down into St James's. He did not speak but
dropped into step at her side, and they strode on in
bitter, suspicious silence through the lazy crowds,
past the ancient and expensive little shops where
single pairs of riding boots, solitary pictures and
astonishingly extravagant neckwear are displayed
to attract the fastidious of two continents, and so on
into the gracious quietude of Sallet Square.

A small army of cameramen caught them as they passed the doorway of the empty house on the corner, and they fled together from it, Frances white with misery and apprehension and David grasping her arm and thrusting her forward, his thin mouth narrowed and his eyes dark. There were several stragglers in the square, silent, mildly inquisitive figures in the dim November gloom who were kept discreetly on the move by a bored police constable. One woman remained in Frances' memory to the end of her days. She stood on the curb, a vast, shapeless figure in a last year's hat, carrying a shopping basket and watching with greedy yet oddly apathetic eyes the shrouded windows of 38, which, like well-bred faces, had nothing to show the world of the wretchedness of fear within.

Miss Dorset met the two in the hall, and the pathetic expression on her face, with the pinched red nose and the watery eyes, broke in upon their private crisis with relieving urgency. Her story was simple and disastrous. Meyrick was held up in Brindisi. The one eventuality which is always possible in Eastern travel but which is somehow never envisaged had occurred. A case of yellow fever had developed on the plane, and the entire company, passengers and crew, had been clapped into quarantine at the Italian port. There was nothing to be done and no help for it. Meyrick was a prisoner for a fortnight at least.

"He sounded so upset on the phone." Disappointment made Miss Dorset's tone plaintive. "He'd just seen the news of Mr Robert's death. I thought he was

going to have a stroke, poor man. What a frightful
home-coming for him!"

Frances looked at her blankly. This extraneous
piece of bad luck coming in the very midst of disaster
seemed to finish everything, and she only realised
then how much she had been relying on Meyrick and
the return of his blessed authority. The secret conviction that it would be all right tomorrow had been
buoying her up, keeping her abreast of the time. Now
she was alone again, rather desperately and painfully
alone.

Miss Dorset's voice addressing David cut into her
thoughts.

"Mrs Madrigal sent down word that you were
going to see to everything with Mr Worthington . . .
that's the solicitor. I'm so glad," she was saying
earnestly. "I'd have done it, of course, but these
things do need a man. I don't know why. It's the
custom, I suppose. I only realised just now that it
would have to be so . . . so quick. The inquest was
adjourned this morning. I don't think Mr Bridie
even troubled to go. He knew what was going to
happen. The pathologist rang up when you were out.
It 'll have to be the day after tomorrow, I'm afraid."

David frowned. Frances saw him standing there,
his hair a little on end and his fine-boned face, which
was so sensitive and yet so masculine, animated with
distaste and pity.

"Oh, the funeral you mean?" he said. "The day
after tomorrow? Really? That's rather hurried, isn't
it?"

"Well, no, not really." Miss Dorset was flushed.
"The . . . er . . . operation has been done and the
pathologist suggested, very nicely of course, that . . . "

Her voice faded and he nodded with sudden
comprehension.

"Of course," he said hurriedly. "I was forgetting.
Very well then, I'll see to it. I'll go down and see
Worthington now. You'll want it very quiet, natu-
rally."

"Oh, I think so. Old Mrs Ivory must be consulted,
but I should think as quiet as possible. I'll go and ask
her, unless you'd like to, Miss Frances?"

"No." Frances spoke with sudden decision. "No,
you go, will you? I'll come up later. I want a word
with Mr Field."

She waited until the woman was out of sight and
the brisk clatter of her heels on the parquet above
had died away before she went into the breakfast
room. He followed her, his hands in his pockets and
his shoulders hunched.

"Phillida asked me, you know," he said. "Someone's got to do it for the poor girl. It's a horrible job."

It was not that the words sounded like an excuse,
and thereby inferred that she needed one. She had put
that personal aspect of the day's sum of trouble resolutely out of her mind. But the remark jarred on her
and she plunged wildly into the awkward statement
she had planned.

"Look here, David," she said, realising that her
cheeks were flushed but unaware that she looked
young and a trifle dishevelled, "this entire business

has got hopelessly out of hand from our point of view. I mean last week, when you were awfully kind and made the terrific gesture, neither of us realised what was coming to us. Wouldn't you like to call the engagement joke off? Even if it made us look silly it would at least clear up a few of the complications. I feel I'm dragging you into this mess, and it's all rather beastly and shame making and will be worse later on."

She was looking at him directly, but after the first word or so he had not met her eyes but had wandered over to the window and now stood staring out through the gauze curtains at the square.

"I think you'd better," she said and waited. She had no idea what she expected of him, no conscious notion that she was being anything but painfully sincere. Her first impression was that he was going to laugh at her, but his complete silence was disconcerting.

"You clear right out of it," she said earnestly. "We're going to be the Piccadilly lepers, I can see that. It's no good being paralysingly decent and sticking by us. You get away while you're uncontaminated."

Again he let her words die in the room and then, while the silence still ticked uncomfortably, shrugged his shoulders.

"I'd like to," he said simply. "There's nothing I feel I'd rather do."

"Well, you go," she said blankly.

He laughed and came over to her.

"Darling," he said, "you're lovely. All elementary and untrodden and violets down the path. No complexes, no inhibitions, just plain unadulterated female youth. It's disgustingly rare and painfully attractive. As a rule this is the point where the old cad packs up. However, look over here."

He took her back to the window and pointed to a solitary figure idling against the railings of the square.

"There he is," he said, "boots and all. If I leave the house he goes too. This is a solemn moment. For the first time in his life the old man is trapped, Duchess."

His hand was on her shoulder and she felt it tighten briefly.

"If he wasn't there you'd go," she said.

"My God, I would," said David Field.

9

TO EVERYONE'S ASTONISHMENT GABRI-
elle put her foot down about the funeral, and in her
decree the great Victorian instinct for social self-
preservation became apparent.

"Quiet?" she demanded, sitting up in her chair as
she did in the afternoons. "At a time like this? Don't
be ridiculous. My dears, we do not admit that there
is any scandal. Our poor wretched relation has died,
and we owe it to ourselves to see him buried in a right
way. Besides, if a few sensation mongers are going to
crowd round the house, for heaven's sake, give them
something to gape at."

She disapproved strongly of David's share in the
arrangements and told him so, but since his name
had already been mentioned to the solicitors she
agreed that "less talk" would arise from his continuing the work than from his being superseded in
it, and she had him and old Worthington, together
with the undertaker, up in her room for the best
part of an hour.

Some of her decisions were out of date, but Frances,
who was appointed her lieutenant in the business,
began to recognise for the first time the awe-inspiring
common sense behind the absurdities of that great

social code of the day before yesterday. She did what
she was told and bought black for herself, Phillida
and every servant in the house, and with Miss Dorset
she sat up late into the night sending "intimations"
and instructions for the despatch of flowers to everyone who might possibly have some claim to be
informed.

The gruesome preparations added to the horror of
the situation by a hundred per cent. Plain-clothes
men on guard outside the house helped to bring
wreaths into the hall, and old Bridie, with his bright
inquisitive eyes popping in their arched sockets,
seemed to move in a perpetual odour of lilies. Startled
dress-shop women with a couple of mannequins
apiece were shown into Gabrielle's bedroom, where
she kept them parading up and down in funereal
splendour until she was satisfied that her granddaughters were to be suitably clad.

Nobody wept. There was a grim purpose in the
proceedings and a strange element of gallantry.

Frances, her arm full of black chiffon, ran into
David outside Phillida's door on the night before
the interment. The entire house reeked like a florist's
shop, and death was far more present in the graceful
building than ever it had been on the morning when
Robert's pathetic corpse had first been discovered
in the garden room.

David was visibly shaken. He looked younger and
more vulnerable and his eyes were shocked.

"It's archaic," he said. "Utterly horrible. My
God, if one had liked the fellow it would have driven

one mad. I say, did you know? They've picked up
Lucar. It's in the stop press tonight. He wired from
mid-Atlantic or something equally preposterous.
It's extraordinary the way the police go about the
house, brushing one on the stairs, nodding to one
in the passages, yet never telling anything. Quite
reasonable, I suppose, but disconcerting. Still, who's
going to worry about Lucar or anyone else while this
is going on? In the ordinary way we'd be hysterical
with excitement, I suppose, but with Grandmamma's
macabre pantomime taking place all round one everything else blurs."

Frances agreed. She was very weary, and in the
last few days the skin had contracted over her fine
bones, leaving her face pointed and fragile. He looked
at her sharply and spoke with a flicker of his old
manner.

"Don't let it get you," he said. "Anyway don't go
all ethereal over it. It's wise, you know. She's absolutely fantastic, but she's dead right. That's the
amazing thing about it. It's sensible. In fact it's
genius. It leaves all the doors open. People who
aren't sure how the cat's going to jump can send
flowers and stay away and so save their faces in any
eventuality. If by a miracle the whole stink blows
over amicable relations can be resumed without
heartburning . . . if it does."

The thought seemed to worry him for he glanced
at Phillida's door and frowned.

"Are you going in to her? I wish you would." His
concern for the other woman was urgent and personal.

Frances imagined that she understood it and felt
again the age-old stab which the Marthas of this
world must always feel when the Marys score their
inevitable triumphs.

David was embarrassed. "I've been with her all
the evening," he said. "Do you know, I don't think
she ought to be left."

"I'll stay with her." Her tone betrayed her and he
glanced behind him. She saw him for a moment with
the visor up. His eyes were helpless and his expression
unexpectedly supplicant.

"Have a heart, Duchess," he said.

Afterwards she realised that they came as near to
understanding one another then as ever before, but
at that moment the door was flung open and a haggard relic of Phillida Madrigal appeared on the
threshold.

"Whispering," she said breathlessly. "Whispering
outside the door. It goes on all the time. I can't stand
it. Can't you come in?"

"My dear, I'm so sorry. I didn't realise how near
we were." Frances turned into the room at once.
"Look here, Gabrielle says . . . " Her words died as
Phillida took the dress from her arms and threw it
across a chair. She was trembling, and the green of
her house coat seemed to have tinged her skin.

"I don't think I shall want an evening dress
again," she said abruptly. "Tell Gabrielle so. Tell
Gabrielle . . . tell Gabrielle . . . " Her mouth trembled
out of control and Frances put an arm round her.

"Sit down," she said firmly. "I'm sorry we stood

talking out there. Never mind about the clothes. Gabrielle's old, you know, and she's fussy. It's a ghastly business, but we've got to get it over somehow."

"Get it over?" Phillida sat huddled in the chair like an old woman, her spine arched under the quilted coat. "Get it over?" she repeated. There was an unnatural weariness in the phrase and Frances glanced at her uneasily.

Outside the wind had risen again. It crept round the house, fitful and mischievous. It was not so boisterous as it had been on that significant night ten days before, but it was the same wind, irritating and uncertain, a living enemy trying to penetrate the fastness of the house.

Frances knelt down before the fire and sat back on her heels, listening to it while it played in and out her thought.

"Whispering," said Phillida suddenly. "Damned whispering everywhere. It's getting on my nerves. I'm growing like Robert, imagining things. Frances, have you ever wished that you were dead? Seriously, I mean, not just saying it. Have you ever sat and wished with all your soul that you'd die or that you had the courage to kill yourself?"

"Yes," said Frances definitely. Her instinct was for caution. "Yes, I have, but not for long. The day goes through it all. Tomorrow night 'll come and the next night. It passes, you know; that's the mercy of it. It doesn't last."

"This will." Phillida was whispering herself, and

for the first time in her life the histrionic effect was
not calculated. "You don't remember 'Dolly,' do
you?"

Frances glanced at her in exasperation. If Phillida
had suddenly decided to mourn for Robert in this
slightly dramatic fashion it might possibly have been
bearable, but to find her preoccupied with a romantic
anxiety was distasteful as well as uncomfortable.

"Yes, I do," she said vaguely.

Phillida shivered. "I remember everything about
him." Her voice was still husky and she had lowered
it until she was hardly intelligible. "He had such
force, Frances, such incredible force. He'll be here
tomorrow. After the funeral the bell will ring and
there 'll be more whispering and steps outside and
he'll be here."

Frances scrambled to her feet.

"You go to bed," she said. "Take some aspirin and
get some sleep. This is madness, my dear. You'll
wear yourself to a rag."

Phillida was not listening to her. Her face looked
ghastly in the bright electric light.

"I'm frightened," she burst out suddenly. "Frightened out of my senses. You can't possibly understand.
Nobody can. Frances, do you think David could
have been in love with me all these years?"

"David?"

"Yes. He was in love with me once. He must have
been. I treated him abominably, I know, but some
men are peculiar when you do that. They get a sort
of respect for you and remember it. If he was a

suppressed sentimental type he might . . . And that
would be too horrible. What should I do? What on
earth should I do?"

"Somehow I shouldn't worry about that." Frances
knew that she sounded brutal and decided that it
could not be helped.

Phillida shook her head.

"It's more than worrying. You don't know," she
said. "Suppose David had known, somehow, that
'Dolly' was going to be found? Suppose he'd had
some sort of psychic intimation? Suppose Robert had
told him, as he told me?" The final words seemed to
frighten her, for she clapped her hands over her
mouth. "I didn't say that!" she burst out like a hysterical child. "I didn't say that. You didn't hear me."

Frances rang the bell.

"I'm going to send for Dorothea and we're putting
you to bed," she announced. "You be quiet and try
to sleep. It's the only thing to do. You'll drive yourself out of your mind if you go on like this."

"You didn't believe what I said?" Phillida was
frankly hysterical.

"I didn't even hear it," said Frances with feeling.
"Do you want a bath, because if you do I'll turn it
on for you?"

Phillida was still crying when they got her into
bed, and old Dorothea sat by her until she slept, but
in the morning, to the relief and astonishment of the
entire household, she pulled herself together. She
came down comparatively early, a graceful grey-
hound figure in her black suit, looked at the flowers

and even let Mrs Sanderson weep to her a little. Frances saw her on that morning standing stiffly by a tremendous wreath from the employees at 39. Her chin was up and her eyes were blank. Even then, before she understood, then, while the whole terrible complication was still unknown to her, she recognised that blind courage and the picture of it sank deep into her mind.

The funeral itself was one of those unbelievable pieces of picturesque nightmare which sometimes slip into real life to remind one that there is nothing so painfully absurd that it cannot happen. To begin with, the wind had risen almost to gale force without losing its fitful quality. It raced round the square, tormenting and blinding, snatching at hats and whipping at skirts, irritating the horses and disarranging the flowers. It was like Gabrielle to insist on horses. No motor hearse in the world can convey the same macabre dignity which six brown-black horses, complete with silver buckles and black plumes, can produce with a single rattle of their well-oiled hoofs. The plumes were the undertaker's own contribution. He was an elderly man who recognised a real Victorian when he met one. Moreover, in company with most of his kind, he deplored the passing of the pomp and circumstance of death. The plumes had been resurrected, therefore, for the first time since the war had given Londoners new and simpler ideas about interment. Now they stood high in their silver sconces on top of the hearse and on the nodding heads of the black horses, looking like bunches of gigantic crepe palm leaves. The wind leapt on them with a squeal of triumph as they waved before the breakfast-room windows, and Robert Madrigal waited for the last time for his friends.

There were few friends. Flowers had arrived by the cartload, but the fashionable crowd was absent. However, there was no dearth of mourners. The newspapers had announced the event. "PICTURE EXPERT MURDER: FUNERAL," said the evening boards in Piccadilly, and the square was full of sober, idle people, not one of whom had so much as nodded to the living Robert but who had come to watch his burying as they would have come to watch any other procession with a bit of a tale to it. They helped considerably, of course. Frances realised that when she came back from the grim, chilly little ceremony and everybody met in the drawing room to thaw and to drink and forget if they could that vast sad cemetery where the flowers had been left to the roistering wind and Robert to the hideous yellow earth.

Here the guests were comparatively few. Most of the staff from 39 was present, of course, as were the usual collection of obscure relatives who always appear at weddings and funerals like some sort of family phenomena, while old Worthington had come, bringing his son, who stood about the doctors, and a decayed gentleman who belonged to Robert's club and had owed him money. But for the rest there were only telegrams and more and more last-minute flowers.

The only uninvited guests in the house were the

police. They hung about shamefully, like bailiffs, grimly amused in their official capacity but as men secretly a trifle overawed. The expedition itself had been preposterous. Since Robert had no relatives nearer than South Africa a Victorian stoicism had decreed that his widow should travel in the first limousine accompanied by a startled old nephew of Gabrielle's own as her escort. He was a pathetic person who had been fetched up from his Bournemouth boarding house by a telegram which was as near blackmail as made no difference, and he had sat huddled in the car beside his kinswoman, trying to remember long-forgotten manners and privately worrying about the draughts and his own weak chest.

Frances herself, with David in his capacity as her fiancé, had gone next, and behind them rode Miss Dorset, supported by the head of the clerical department from the gallery.

It had been a brave show, as formal and courageous as Gabrielle herself. Mrs Ivory's ultimate act of gallantry was her personal appearance in the drawing room. She was waiting for them when they came in, enthroned in the largest of the wing chairs with Dorothea, like a sentinel, behind her. She was completely in black, a colour she had always detested, and from the shrouding folds her face and hands shone out as pale and polished as her name.

Lawrence's full-length portrait of Philip Ivory as a young man smiled down at her, and the light from the lustres which had seen her in her glory picked up the folds of her moiré skirt. As a spectacle she took a lot

of beating, and the unhappy company, in whose mind
the words "mystery," "something queer," "scandal," "murder," were taking larger and larger space,
turned to her with admiration and relief.

Yet it was not easy. Everyone in the room felt the
same sense of responsibility, the same sensation of
herding together in the face of disaster, while beneath
this there was that other feeling, the sneaking sensa-
tionalism which murmurs, "This may be an un-
forgettable experience. Who knows, I may be rubbing
shoulders with a murderer at his victim's funeral."

As the sunburst clock over the mantelshelf ticked
the seconds by this last thought grew more and more
general, until it could almost be seen flitting from
mind to mind. All round the room people would fall
silent, blank expressions on their faces, uneasy excitement in their eyes, as they glanced round covertly
over their cups and glasses. "Who?" whispered the
thought. "Who had a motive? Who are the police
watching? Who killed him?"

Frances was with Gabrielle when Norris came in.
The old lady had both her granddaughters near her.
Phillida, looking as if she were on the verge of col-
lapse, sat in a chair only a trifle smaller than Mrs
Ivory's own, while Frances stood on the other side.
She realised that they must make a fantastic little
group and was relieved when David came up behind
her.

"Just like the family album. You've no idea," he
murmured. "Want a drink?"

"A small prussic acid, please." She let the flippancy

escape her without taking her eyes from the door. Norris was worming his way towards them. He looked anxious.

He spoke very quietly and yet everyone seemed to hear him. Godolphin. The name fled round the room as audibly as if he had screamed it aloud, and it snatched attention from the one all-absorbing but unfortunately unmentionable topic which was concerning the company. They pounced on it, and the general interest flared.

Godolphin, whose sensational story of his escape from death was even now flooding the newspapers in parallel columns with the latest news from Sallet Square? Godolphin, who had crept out on a ledge of icebound rock to die rather than jeopardise the chances of his companions' safety? Godolphin, who had been discovered on the point of death by a party of monks and carried up by them to a fortress which hitherto had been no more than a legend? Godolphin, who had been a prisoner for close to four years, to escape at last with a pilgrim train? Godolphin himself outside? Really? Godolphin, *the* Godolphin, actually present in the house? Here was romance; here was warmth; here was colour!

Frances caught a glimpse of David's grey face and saw his eyes turn to Phillida, but she was hidden in the depths of her chair, and even then the younger girl had no inkling of the great obvious fact which rose up so monstrously before her eyes that it escaped her altogether.

Norris went out again, and this time the crowd

made a path and stood looking at the tall door covered by the silk portiere curtain with the Chinese panel. Memory is an unaccountable possession, and Frances, who until that moment had had only a hazy impression of the explorer, now received a clear vision of him as she had seen him last five years before. He had been a gaunt whirlwind of a man, not particularly tall but thick-boned and sturdy, with a shock of very black hair standing on end above an eagle nose and narrow eyes. She looked for him with interest when Norris reappeared, stepping back to hold the door open while a flutter of anticipation passed over the gathering.

There was a long pause, and then into the room, blinking a little because of the light, and clad unconventionally in a tweed travelling suit, came a small, withered, elderly man, walking with a stick.

It was not altogether an anticlimax. Many people present remembered Godolphin before his last trip, and David's single muttered expletive expressed their reaction.

Godolphin came uncertainly down the room towards them, and their first impression receded a little. It *was* Godolphin. The much-photographed face was recognisable under the harsh yellow skin, but the hair was white and close cropped and he stooped with the weakness of a man who has undergone a great physical hardship.

He came up to Gabrielle and bent over her hand with a touch of his old bombast.

"Forgive me," he said gently in the rather high

metallic voice which Frances had forgotten. "I didn't know. Your man told me the news on the doorstep. I'm just off the plane. I haven't seen a paper or spoken to a soul. I came straight to Phillida, naturally."

Fortunately he was speaking softly, and the crowd, remembering its manners, made hasty conversation. Only the old woman and the four who surrounded her heard him clearly.

Gabrielle looked up.

"Naturally?" she enquired abruptly. "Why 'naturally,' Mr Godolphin?"

He turned to Phillida, and the movement of his outstretched hand had a quality of finality and homecoming about it.

"It's still a secret, is it, my dear?" he said gently.

Phillida whim red. There was no other word for that dreadful animalic little sound. She was straining back in her chair as if she would force herself into the upholstery.

A bewildering thought struck Frances and she looked at Gabrielle. The old woman was rigid, her black eyes contracted into slits of startling intelligence. It was only then that the youngest Ivory recognised the truth, and with it the appalling explanation of a dozen mysteries of the past unbearable week. The facts came thundering into her mind with the force of revelation. Phillida had married him. Phillida must have married Godolphin before the Tibetan expedition, and now, as he stood smiling before them, Godolphin knew no more about Robert than that he was dead.

10

THE DRAWING ROOM LOOKED DESPOILED
as rooms do when a crowd has recently departed from
them. Even the brilliance of the lustres looked dishevelled and a trifle soiled. Also it was very lonely
and quiet, while the smell of the flowers which still
hung about the house was heavy and unpleasant.

Outside the wind was at its fidgety worst, and to
Frances at least the memory of those days was ever
afterwards accompanied by the mischievous music of
that irritating, ill-tempered breeze.

The old Gabrielle sat huddled in her chair by the
graceful fireplace with the fluted columns. She looked
so old that it seemed incredible that there should still
be sufficient blood in her body to feed the intricate
experienced brain behind her shrewd eyes. One small
hand picked at the thick silk skirt which fell stiffly
over her knees, but apart from this movement she
showed no sign of agitation or even of life.

David leant against the mantelpiece, watching her,
with Frances at his feet on the hearthrug. She sat
with her knees drawn under her, her black dress
making her look younger than ever in spite of the
new maturity which was etching itself upon her face.

The fourth member of the party remained ex-

pressionless. Dorothea stood behind her mistress like
a soldier behind his king. Her face was blank and no
one in the world could have deduced what thoughts,
if any, were passing behind that strong, stupid and
infinitely stoical exterior.

Phillida and Godolphin had been alone in the
breakfast room for forty minutes now. The walls were
thick and no sound had escaped to give the little
gathering waiting in the drawing room any indication
of the way in which that grimly dramatic interview
progressed. There was nothing, only silence and the
blank door.

Everyone deferred to Gabrielle. She had insisted
that they stay beside her, and if it was obvious
that she was keeping them under her eye so that they
should not talk too much among themselves it was
also clear that she was controlling the situation by a
terrific effort of will power alone. Meanwhile the
silence was nerve racking.

David took out his cigarette case, looked at it and
put it back again. Gabrielle eyed him.

"You knew about this," she said. It was not a
question, and he did not deny it.

"Yes," he said. The lazy, tolerant expression had
crept back into his face, but for the first time Frances
wondered how much of it was protective covering.
"Yes, I did. I was a witness at the wedding. It was
when I was over here last time, about four years ago.
I'd been seeing Phillida quite a lot, as you may remember." He looked down at Frances. "You were at
school," he said.

Gabrielle shut her lips tightly, but if he noticed the gesture he ignored it and went on speaking, half to her and half to Frances, choosing his words with a sort of deliberate carelessness, allowing a touch of flippancy to lighten the bleakness of the story.

"Phillida phoned me one day and told me she was getting married, but that it was to be all done in secret. 'Dolly' was broke, or something equally undesirable. She asked me if I'd go along and support them at the ordeal. I did. I was the only friend of bride or groom at the Registry Office, and I signed my name and wished 'em luck. I went back to the States a couple of days later and the next I heard of Godolphin was that he had died out in the wilds on this expedition. I gathered from the press accounts that there'd been no mention of his marriage so I took it that the whole affair was washed out. Then when I came back a few weeks ago I found that Phillida had married Robert and naturally I held my tongue because it was her affair and not mine, and since 'Dolly' was dead there was nothing in it. However, last week, when the whole situation blew sky-high, I did come to see her and I offered her my heartfelt advice, which was to get hold of 'Dolly' quickly and break the news as gently as possible before he got back and someone else told him. Unfortunately, when she did have an opportunity on the transcontinental phone she funked it. One can't really blame the poor girl, but it was a pity. It would have saved this ghastly tragicomedy this afternoon anyway."

There was silence again after he had spoken.

Gabrielle rocked herself to and fro, her eyes narrowed and her mouth twisting to fit unuttered words. Frances stared into the fire. David's laconic account of the secret wedding had not deceived her. During the last few days she had learnt enough about love and enough about people to clothe that skeleton story. She understood now why he had been so cautious when she had coupled Phillida and Godolphin in her first conversation with him in the Café Suprême, and she recognised the reason for his faint air of responsibility where Phillida was concerned. Behind his lazy voice she had caught a glimpse of the cruel if childish gesture of the two adventurers when they had decided to honour the unsuccessful boy friend with their secret. No doubt his presence had lent the occasion just the extra touch of piquancy so dear to their fey postwar generation. It must all have been very young and dramatic and for David unhappy and humiliating if also educational.

She looked up at him and found him watching her, half amused by his own embarrassment. He looked away at once.

"It's a fine old mess now, anyway," he said. "Pelion piled on Ossa. Where do we go from here?"

"She didn't ought to be worried." The passionate ungrammatical statement bursting from Dorothea startled everybody as violently as if a peaceful hill had suddenly decided to erupt without warning. Her large ugly face was suffused with blood, but her wooden expression remained and she shut her mouth as if a zipper fastener had held it.

Gabrielle laughed. It was the first sound of the kind that the house had heard for a week, and the room itself seemed to lighten.

"How true," she said. "That's very kind of you, Dorothea. Very kind, very intelligent, but not helpful. Mr Field, I never in my life allowed anyone to smoke in this room, but now if you want one you may light a cigarette."

David did not smile but he thanked her and took out his case.

The nerve-racking waiting continued. The entire house seemed to be listening, shut up inside itself with the wind ferreting and twittering round the walls.

"He'll have to see reason," said Frances suddenly. "It's an impossible business, and Godolphin will have to be reasonable. After all, it's quite clear how the thing happened."

"Hush." Gabrielle raised a small yellow hand. "Listen, they're coming."

They blinked at her. Her uncannily acute hearing in this house which she knew so well was always astonishing. It was almost a sixth sense with her, depending on a complicated system of old memories and instincts rather than an actual sound. She had raised her head and now turned stiffly in her chair.

She was right, of course. Almost immediately the inner door which connected the breakfast room with the eastern end of the drawing room jarred as the handle turned vigorously and Godolphin appeared. He looked back over his shoulder.

"Come on," he said. "They're all here."

He held the door wide open but there was no sign of Phillida, and presently he disappeared again, to return a moment or so later leading her by the hand. They made an extraordinary pair coming across the rose-pink Chinese carpet together. Godolphin had lost much of the withered, broken appearance which had so shocked them on his first arrival. Whatever else the interview had done it had certainly stimulated him. There was animation in his movements now, and a great wave of nervous energy swept into the room with him, reminding them that he was still a personality. It occurred to Frances for the first time that he might be very angry.

Phillida drooped. She looked utterly exhausted. Her dark lids hung over dull eyes and her arms swung loosely.

David pulled up a chair for her, and Godolphin lowered her into it. His manner was possessive and authoritative, and the old Gabrielle, who was watching him with lynx eyes, let her hands flutter in her lap.

"Well?" she said. It was a grim word, so much better than any conventional condolence or excuse, and Godolphin, who had had his back to her, turned with quick interest as he recognised a personality.

"It's ghastly," he said, his thin high voice snapping out the words. "Horrible. A great shock for you all . . . Not a comforting story for me. There's only one thing to be done. I've been explaining that to my wife. We must all pull together, get this mystery cleared up and then she and I must start afresh."

He made an alarmingly important figure standing before them, his dried flesh clinging to his bones and his whipcord face so thin that the double line of his jaw stuck out in high relief. The shock had told on him. He was leaning heavily on his stick, a quivering bundle of taut nerves.

"Oh, but how sensible." The old Gabrielle used an ingratiating tone which none of them had heard from her before. "You're quite right, of course, Mr Godolphin. The police must be left to make their enquiry into Robert's death, and any mystery there must be settled utterly and beyond question before any other . . . adjustment can be considered. Until that is done you will keep away from Phillida and from this house, naturally. What will you do? Go abroad again?"

He raised his head, and they thought for a moment that he was going to laugh.

"No, dear lady," he said. "I've just spent two years in a filthy lamasery jail, or correction cell as they are pleased to call it, thinking of my home and my wife, and believe me I'm not going to lose either of them again."

His final words clattered in the silent room, and the old woman stiffened visibly.

"I see," she said quietly. "And so what do you suggest?"

"That we get on with the work at once and see the whole hopeless mess settled." He spoke briskly, nervous irritability lending his words a faint contempt.

"That's the only thing to do. The entire affair must be taken in hand at once and, since it affects me principally, I'll do it myself."

Phillida gripped the arms of her chair and struggled to control her voice.

"He doesn't understand," she said helplessly. "He wants to stay in the house."

"That, of course, is impossible." Gabrielle spoke flatly and without intonation in her brittle voice.

"I don't think so." Godolphin was equally decisive. "You're all approaching this thing from the wrong angle. Here you are, a houseful of women completely at the mercy of the police. Your solicitor appears to be worse than useless. Field can't do much because he has no authority and isn't even a permanent resident in the country. You must have somebody to manage things. Frankly, my instinct is to take Phillida out of this and let people say and think what they damned well like, but she won't have that and I can see her point of view. I realise I've come back at an awkward moment in one way, but I feel my arrival is providential in another. There's absolutely no reason why I shouldn't stay here as a guest and do what I can to clear things up. After all, I bring a fresh mind to it and I'm not hampered by the silly conventional mind tracks of this so-called civilised country."

"But my dear chap"—even David was forced to protest—"use your imagination. I know the whole thing is a bit of a mouthful for you to have to swallow but, good heavens, 'Dolly,' think: however un-

pleasant the realisation is, don't ignore what has
happened. Phillida married Robert in all good faith,
and he, poor chap, is only barely in his grave."

Godolphin turned on him. He was trembling and
the veins at the sides of his forehead were prominent.

"I do realise that," he said. "My God, that's the
one thing I do realise."

It was the first open sign of anger which he had
revealed and it sent a thrill of apprehension through
each of them.

Godolphin laughed abruptly.

"I'm sorry," he said, "but you forget. Where I've
been rotting slowly out of existence the niceties have
been absent. I've come back with a clear mind. I'm
not deterred by a pack of half-baked oughts and
ought-nots. I don't care if a thing's good form or even
if it's socially dangerous. I want to take Phillida
away. She's my wife, remember, not Robert's, and
if she won't or can't come away with me until this
blasted mystery's cleared up then I'll clear up the
mystery, and no one on God's earth shall get in my
way. Is that plain enough?"

Nobody spoke. Phillida was crying openly and her
shuddering breath was the only sound in the big
room.

Godolphin confronted Gabrielle.

"If you won't have me in the house, Mrs Ivory,"
he said, "I'll stay in the nearest hotel, but if you've
any sense you'll use me, not frustrate me."

The old woman considered him, her bright eyes
frankly speculative.

"Thank you for your offer," she said with surprising meekness. "Yes, Mr Godolphin, we shall be very pleased if you will consider yourself my son's guest for a few days." She paused and smiled at him. "You will behave like a guest, of course?"

For an instant they regarded each other steadily, both of them adventurers in their way, and presently he laughed.

"You're very wise," he said. "Yes, I'll behave."

The old Gabrielle sighed, a sound of resignation. Then she withdrew into the depths of her high chair.

"I am very tired," she remarked and went on talking in a detached fashion which reminded Frances of her interview in the Hampstead house. "No, Dorothea, I'll come presently but not yet. First of all there is something I have to say to all of you. You need not listen to me if you do not want to, but you are all in my drawing room where I have every right to say what I like, and it is polite to listen to me. First of all I am an old woman. I am so old that half the time my mind wanders abominably, but usually in the evenings it becomes very clear, and just at this particular time I think I may be seeing things more vividly than any of you, because I have one great advantage. I am apart. My life is at its end. My emotions are dead already and I do not care very much what happens to me or to anybody else. I do not know if you realise it, but although some of you are my grandchildren you are all strangers to me. You are not only out of my generation but out of my span. I am looking at you from a long way off."

She was leaning back, infinitely frail in a barricade
of stiff black silk. Her hands were folded placidly and
if her performance had an ulterior motive, as Frances,
who had seen one or two of them, was inclined to
suspect, it was certainly tremendously impressive.
In a second she had withdrawn from them, left them,
washed her hands of them and had retired into a
sanctuary made of time itself.

"As I see it you have all developed one great weakness during the past hour," she remarked, a hint of
complacency in her tinkling voice. "You have all
got a secret now which somehow or other you must
keep from the police. Before this afternoon Phillida
had that secret and so had Mr Field. Now Frances
knows it and so does Dorothea, and I know it."

She paused and looked at Godolphin, who was
staring at her incredulously.

"And so do you," she said. "Now, when the police
talk to you you must all be very careful. The standard
of intelligence among the police is far higher than I
had supposed." There was a world of unconscious
snobbery in the final observation, and they realised
that she had probably never spoken to a policeman
before in her life.

"Do you know, I don't think it matters." Godolphin made the announcement with the force and
recklessness which had been noticeable in him ever
since his interview with Phillida. "The police are
sensible people. They want to know the truth and so
do we. We must work with them; not against them.
They'll want to know the facts of this marriage

mix-up, and I don't see why they shouldn't have . them. I'm against secrets. If we hadn't kept our marriage a secret this wretched complication would never have cropped up. My death would have to have been proved, or Phillida would have to have waited for seven years or whatever the period is before she could have presumed it. I say tell the police. There can't be much of a row. As far as I can find out from Phillida poor old Robert must have died last Monday week, just about the time when I was lying under a mass of stinking goatskins, being smuggled over the border in a mule train. As Robert died I came to life. Phillida never had two husbands at once, so where's the immorality? Let them thresh it all out. They won't prosecute her for bigamy. They're not lunatics. While she was married to Robert I *was* dead to all practical purposes. The police are human and reasonable, surely."

"Oh no, 'Dolly,' no. Don't tell." They had half forgotten Phillida, and her panic-stricken appeal startled them. She was leaning forward. "Don't tell them," she said. "You don't know. You don't understand. Robert was queer before he died, awfully queer and sort of psychic. I used to think he'd guessed about you and me. For the last year he'd talked about you to all sorts of people. He talked to you about him, didn't he, David?"

"To me?" David seemed surprised. "No," he said cautiously. "No, I don't think he did."

"Oh well, he did to me. He did. He talked and talked. Sometimes I was sure he knew about the marriage. He tortured me, I tell you. This last six months has been hell, absolute hell."

Old Mrs Ivory refolded her hands and her eyes rested on Godolphin's face.

"There, you see," she said placidly. "Phillida should not be allowed to talk, should she?"

"Why not?" Godolphin was vigorously rational. "Anyone can see what happened there. Robert happened to mention my name by chance one day and that started up the poor girl's guilty conscience. Since she was nervy anyway and underoccupied it turned into a neurosis. Look at her, poor darling. She's a mass of hysteria now and must have been for months."

Gabrielle beckoned Dorothea.

"You can take me up now," she said and added, shooting at Godolphin a glance so direct that it took him out of his stride and brought the whole company up with a jerk as they stared into the pit she revealed to them, "The police are so unimaginative, my dear man. That's why you must be so careful. Given that story they might almost consider that poor Phillida had a motive, mightn't they?"

11

IT WAS RAINING WHEN MISS DORSET TOOK
up the squalling telephone from among the piles of
scattered papers on her desk. It had been raining for
the best part of a week and the square was cold and
sodden. The black branches of the trees dripped
sooty tears onto the forlorn grass. The morning-paper
boards, which for the first time for days bore no
reference to the mystery, were soaking and disrepu-
table.

She approached the instrument cautiously. Just
lately some of the calls had not been pleasant experiences.

"Hello," she said briskly. "Hello. Who? Oh yes,
Miss Dorset speaking. Yes, of course I remember
you. You're Mr Lucar's man, aren't you? I'm afraid
I haven't any news for you yet. I should just carry
on as I told you."

"Wait a minute, miss." The bright cockney voice
was knowing. "You've slipped past yerself. I've got
a bit of news for you. I've 'eard from my guv'nor."

"Have you?" Her surprise escaped her and he
laughed contentedly.

"I know. It took me back a bit, an' that's a fact.
I'd got it well in my 'ead that 'e'd given me the
walkout. Milk's not paid, nor papers, nor my wages.

I was certain I'd said good-bye to that lot, which was why I got on to your firm. They employed 'im, I thought, so per'aps they'd see to me."

"Yes, yes, so you said. You've heard from him, you say?"

"I 'ave. A wire from a ship. It's just come. I'll read it to you. Are you there? Listen. 'Expect me sleep flat tonight, Lucar.'" There was a faint sardonic chuckle. "Sure of 'isself, ain't 'e?"

"He is! I mean, of course." Miss Dorset floundered and recovered herself. "Oh well then, if he's coming back you're all right, aren't you? Thank you for telling me."

"Not at all." The voice was cocky. "I thought you'd like to know. I never thought 'e done it. I told you. I say, you there?"

"Yes. Thank you very much for ringing. Good ..."

"Don't want to discuss it, eh?"

"No, I'm afraid I don't. But thank you for ringing. Good-bye."

"That's all right. I don't blame you. So long."

Miss Dorset replaced the receiver and sat looking in front of her with introspective eyes. Mechanically she took up an envelope from the pile to her left and slit the cheap paper open. After a glance at the opening sentence she pitched the lightly scribbled page into the basket, unread. Stretching out for the next packet, her hand wavered and she took up the telephone instead and dialled 38's number. She got Frances immediately. It was almost as though she had been waiting for a call.

"Hello. Oh, it's you, Miss Dorset?" The dis-appointment was well suppressed. "How are you getting on? Are there many of them?"

"A few." Miss Dorset considered the littered desk with distaste. "I thought I'd better go through them myself. It's not that I don't trust anyone else but it's not a pleasant job, and if it got on a junior clerk's nerves one couldn't blame him for talking. I really didn't know there were so many lunatics at large. It's having an address in the reference books, I suppose. Anyone can get hold of it. If they'd sign their names it wouldn't be so bad. There are one or two genuine personal letters for Mrs Madrigal, by the way. I'll send those over."

"It's abominable, isn't it?" Frances' voice was savage over the wire. "Don't people realise they can't know the truth just by reading a few beastly newspapers? All the letters are for Phillida, are they?"

"Yes, most of them."

"Any for me?"

"One or two." Miss Dorset eyed the solid heap on the right-hand side of the desk and hoped she might be forgiven.

"What do they say?"

"Oh, nothing really. Just abuse. It's purely patho-logical. I asked Inspector Bridie and he says it always happens. 'Chust chealousy and spite,' he said."

Frances laughed unnaturally. "I like him," she said, "or at least I would if I wasn't so afraid of him."

"Afraid?"

"Oh, not seriously. I mean it's all practically settled now, isn't it? Or it will be as soon as they bring Lucar back, won't it?"

The words were belied by the urgent question in the tone, and Miss Dorset's face grew anxious.

"I should think so, my dear." Long years of discretion taught her voice just the right degree of noncommittal cheerfulness. "One or two of these anonymous letters to Mrs Madrigal mention Mr Godolphin. I don't like to say anything to her myself, but people do remember that they were once engaged and it does give them such a handle. He's still determined to stay in the house, is he?"

"I'm afraid he is." It was Frances' turn to be cautious, but her irritation betrayed her. "He's so keen. He works like a fiend. It's like having a policeman present at every meal."

Miss Dorset coughed.

"That kind of person is very trying but they're also very useful sometimes," she said. "They've got such energy. They go on ferreting until they do get to the truth."

"Yes, I know."

There was a brief pause.

"I haven't seen Mr Field for a day or two." In her effort to make the question casual it sounded to Miss Dorset herself that she underlined it unmercifully.

"No," said Frances. "No. Nor have I. You'll send the genuine letters over then, will you?"

"Yes, I will. Good-bye. Is Mrs Ivory all right?"

"Amazingly well. Good-bye."

Ten minutes later the phone in the breakfast room at 38 tinkled again, but when Frances leapt on it she was just in time to hear the soft click on the wire which meant that someone else in the house had also expected a call, and Phillida's nervous voice said urgently:

"Is that Doctor Smith now? This is Mrs Madrigal. Is that Doctor Smith's house? Well, can I speak to him? Put me through. Put me through, please. Put me through."

Frances hung up, and across the city a nurse grimaced as she handed the instrument to a thin man with a tired face who took it wearily.

"No," he said gently after the phone had crackled at him for a full minute. "No, my dear lady, how can I? We threshed all this out yesterday. Why don't you do what I tell you? Go to bed and stay there with a book. Yes, I will. I'll come and see you about four o'clock, but please don't ask me to do the impossible."

"Why not?" Phillida was unusually decisive. "It wouldn't matter. Really it wouldn't matter. I *was* in my room all that day. I didn't go down except once when old Mrs Ivory came over in the afternoon. Why shouldn't you say I couldn't move?"

"Because it's not true."

"Does that matter so much?"

"Do you expect me to answer that question?"

"No. No. I don't know. I'm sorry. I'm mad. I'm ill. I don't know what I'm doing. You won't tell anyone I asked you?"

"I'm not unprofessional as a rule."

"I know you're not. I didn't mean that. Come and see me."

"Yes, I will. This afternoon. Meanwhile take three of the tablets and go to bed. Would you like to go into a nursing home?"

"I would. Oh, I would! Do you think it would look as though I were running away? No, I'd better not. No. You won't do that little thing I asked you? I could sleep if you promised."

"I will not. I'll come and see you this afternoon. Good-bye."

"And yet I don't believe it," he continued to the nurse as she hung up for him. "That woman's a neurasthenic, not a maniac. If she killed her husband I'll eat my brass plate and go and keep chickens."

"I wonder you don't keep away from her all the same," said the nurse practically. "No one, not even a man with your reputation, can afford to be mixed up in that sort of thing."

"You're horribly right," he agreed gloomily, "but I'm sorry for her. You don't know her, do you? She's got a certain charm."

At this precise moment Detective Sergeant Randall of the N Division was standing in a public telephone booth on a dreary wind-swept railway station talking to Divisional Detective Inspector Bridie.

"Got him, sir," he reported briefly.

"Ye have, have ye? Cholly good. What's he like?"

"Cocky, sir."

"Ah, he is? I thought that would be likely. Bring him along."

"Right, sir. The train goes in seven minutes. We'll be with you before five."

The Orkney man grunted and hung up. The brief conversation appeared to have pleased him considerably, for he decided to treat himself to one of his rare cigarettes. He selected it with care from the box on his office desk. It was an unexpectedly pansy affair with a filter and a hygienic mouthpiece. Strangers were apt to regard this uncharacteristic taste in tobacco with astonishment, but those who knew him best were inclined to attribute it to native canniness and a naïve attempt to temper the vice of smoking with the off chance that the beastly things were doing him good.

He smoked half the cylinder with earnest preoccupied enjoyment and would doubtless have gone on until the fumes of the burning filter choked him, as he usually did, had he not been interrupted by a thought. He took up the house phone and got through to Inspector Withers, a placid, painstaking man in whom he had great faith.

"Any results?" he enquired, cocking his head on one side at the mouthpiece.

"A blank . . . sir." Withers added the courtesy as an afterthought. The two men were friends but he was in a bad temper. "I've been through every perishing report, forty-seven of 'em. No nigger for miles. Not a soul in or about those two houses on the night in question saw hide or hair of a nigger except those two hysterical women."

"No." The inspector conveyed that he did not presume to argue.

Bridie sniffed. "Mrs Sanderson may be an emotional pairson," he conceded, "and mebbe the girl Molly is not par-rticularly strong in the heid, but when those two women say they saw a nigger walk past the kitchen window into the yar-rd chust before dusk that day I was inclined to believe them."

Silence.

"I tek it you cholly well weren't?"

"No, I was not, sir." Withers was still polite but it was with an effort. "I'm sorry, but a more cockeyed tale I never laid ears to. Why didn't they raise cain at the time?"

"Because the yar-rd was in chuxtaposition to the picture gallery next door, and strange pairsons were forever walking down there."

"I see. Well, if that's so why wasn't this blinking nigger likely to be one of the . . . er . . . strange pairsons with a right to be there? Fetching a packing case or something. Why bother about him?"

"Because he had no right to be there. No one knew of him. Ye say so yourself, man."

Withers remained unimpressed. "I'll go on following it up, of course," he said.

"That's right," agreed Bridie with exasperating satisfaction.

"Any luck in your other direction?" The inspector could not restrain the gentle dig and Bridie smiled affectionately at the instrument.

"I'm keeping an eye on the lad," he said comfortably. "He's stayin' away from the hoose and amusin' himself, but we'll let him bide for an hour or two. He's costing the country a mint in shoe leather but it can't be helped." With which cryptic announcement he hung up and returned to his cigarette, now nearly burnt through, he noted with regret.

Meanwhile in another room in the same building a charge sergeant was being severe over the telephone. "I can't help who you are, sir," he was saying, "but you've been on the chief twice today already and unless you have some new information, in which case you can report it to me first, I can't put you through to him again. Everything is being done, you can rest assured of that."

"That's all very well, but is it?" Godolphin did not sound amused. "It's over a fortnight now, you know, and the inquest will be resumed in less than six days."

"We know that, sir. We're working on the case." The sergeant listened attentively and sighed as he heard the explorer hang up. "He thinks he's doing his duty, you know," he remarked tolerantly to the constable who leant against the desk. "That's the funny thing. You always find it in a bloke who's been out East. Stirrin' 'em up, they call it among themselves. It's all right for foreigners, but back 'ere it's just fidgeting. You notice it in old army men."

At three in the afternoon Miss Frances Ivory very hurriedly, and with a palpably fictitious explanation ready on her lips, rang up the studio flat in St John's Wood which Pendlebury, the R.A., had let to David

Field for the winter. She stood listening to the bell
ringing and ringing in the empty room for a long time
after she realised that had anyone been there he
must have answered it, and she returned to the
deserted drawing room, mingled irritation and relief
tempering the breathless feeling of despair which had
brought her to much weakness.

A little later in the day, when Phillida was with
her doctor, when Frances was still hovering near the
telephone, when Bridie was reading the second report
of the day on David Field's itinerary, when Miss
Dorset was burning a basketful of scurrilous filth in
the basement furnace at the gallery, when Godolphin
was preparing his third list of questions for Norris to
answer and when Henry Lucar, his red hair blazing
above his pallid face, was riding in a London-bound
train with Sergeants Randall and Betts in attendance,
a very queer conversation passed over the wires
between one small house in Tooting and another on
the far side of London in Cricklewood.

"I saw her, Mum," said a young voice in Tooting.

"What did she say?" The older voice in Cricklewood was nervous.

"She said she couldn't. She knew you was right but
she couldn't. She can't leave her lady since she's so
old. She might die without her, she said."

"I dare say she would, but that can't be helped
when there's one's self to think of. I do think she
might think of her relations and what people say.
Did you tell her it wasn't very nice for her own sister,
living a respectable life, to be pointed out as a person

connected with the murder? Some people might
enjoy it, I dare say, but not our family. We're respectable and we're Chapel and always have been.
Did you tell her that?"

"I told her, Mum."

"And still she said she couldn't leave?"

"That's what she said."

"Did you tell her Dad and I would have her here
if we had to?"

"Yes, Mum, I told her, but she wouldn't come."

"She is aggravating. She always was. Obstinate as
a pig."

There was a pause and then the same voice went
on again, lowered this time.

"Did she say anything about it?"

"No, nothing, except that she didn't know 'oo'd
done it."

"Oh." The old voice was disappointed. "Dad
feels we ought to hear as soon as anybody."

"Yes." The younger voice sounded preoccupied
and presently became impulsive. "Mum? I say, I
think she's mixed up in it."

"*She* is?"

"I think so."

"Oh. Oh, my God. Never let your father hear that.
What did she say? She didn't say she'd done it?"

"No, of course not. She didn't say nothing reely.
I only felt she knew something. She knows something
and isn't saying. I come away . . . "

The last relevant telephone call of the day was put
through at six-thirty in the evening. David Field

rang 38 Sallet Square. Frances answered him and was
so relieved to hear him at last that her own voice
betrayed her.

"Hello, Duchess, is that you?" He sounded irritatingly normal. "How are you?"

"All right."

"Are you? Is that the truth or are you being the
gallant little woman?"

"I'm being gallant."

He laughed with spontaneous pleasure.

"Are you, darling? I bet you are. Will you come
out and eat with me tonight? Yes, I know, but wait
a moment. I particularly want you to come, and I'll
choose a place where the chances are that we shan't
meet anyone who has ever seen us before. Don't
worry. Film stars wander round London without
being recognised. Don't get a neurosis about publicity."

"I don't want to come," she said, adding casually,
"Can't you take somebody else?"

"Of course I can. I rather thought we ought to
meet, though. I haven't been round for a day or so,
and a gossip writer phoned me this morning to ask
if our engagement was still on."

"Oh. What did you say?"

"Me? I was very upstage. Wasn't that right? I
said indeed it was and if I read anything to the contrary in his perishing column I should be happy to
sue him or kick his seat for him, whichever he pre-
ferred. Put on a nice blue dress and I'll fetch you at
seven-thirty."

"Gabrielle says we're all to wear black for a month."

"Does she indeed? I say, I like her. Old Grandmamma Intestinal Fortitude, isn't she? Have you got a mourning dance garment?"

"Yes."

"Fine. Seven-thirty then. Hold your head up. By the way, I shall come in a humble cab. No Daimlers. What did you say?"

"I said I should hope so. David?"

"Yes."

"Why haven't you been round?"

"Eh?"

"Why haven't you been round?"

She heard him laugh again, awkwardly this time.

"Oh, funk, you know," he said and rang off, leaving her wondering.

12

THE MARBLE HALL WAS SO NAMED BY ITS
astute proprietor out of deference to that variety of
self-derision which has been the very essence of chic
ever since the first postwar generation grew up. It
was a large comfortable night club and restaurant,
designed for those wary birds, the intelligentsia of
the smart set, and had actually succeeded in captur-
ing a great many of them. It was outrageously expensive, comparatively exclusive, and it was also,
as somebody said of it on the opening night, pleasant
without being in any way good. The *décor* was
slavishly of the nineties, and one of its great features
was the row of little ornamental boxes built in round
the unusually narrow balcony where diners could
indulge in a little ostentatious discretion. The looped
red curtains drawn well back contrived to defeat
their avowed object by calling attention to those who
sat framed in them, so everyone was content and the
original joke preserved.

The ground-floor tables, huddled round the tiny
dancing ring, were crowded when Frances came in
with David, but one was reserved for them, and they
sat down in the shadow of a ridiculous palm.

He watched her for a minute or two, his eyes
narrowed professionally.

"All Degas," he said. "Lovely. I like the dress. It's just right in this studied pretentiousness. Don't look round like a hunted fawn or something. That's carrying the jest too far. Don't worry. There's not a soul in this room who can spare a second to recognise anyone but themselves. That's the strength of this age. Individualism."

It was always like this, she reflected. She met him in a painful overwrought state of nerves, suspicion and self-consciousness, and in five minutes he soothed and bullied her into easy friendliness with a gentle if far too experienced hand. He had turned from her and was looking up at the boxes with interest, so that she had plenty of time to see that he was thinner and to notice the underlying nervous strength which kept his manner so light and controlled. He was an odd person.

They had barely finished the meal when the message came. David took the note from the waiter's tray, and the corners of his wide mouth turned down as he read it.

"Spotted," he remarked. "Come on, lady. This is where you hold my hand."

"What is it? What's happened?"

"Hey . . . " He paused in the act of rising to peer at her. "Keep your hands on the wheel. I didn't know you were going like this. I thought you were all ice and steel, like the girls in the books out of ships' libraries. It's all right. We're only going to see Uncle Adolphus having a sleuth's night out."

He took her by the elbow, and they followed the

waiter up the grand staircase which was so archly
"amusing" with its red plush and white painted
ironwork, and down the narrow mirror-lined corridor
behind the dining booths. The man knocked and held
a door open for them.

Their first impression was of mellowness and
candlelight. The curtains had been partially drawn,
and the small dining table set far back in the box.
Their principal emotion, however, was frank old-
fashioned consternation. "Dolly" Godolphin, looking very spruce and self-important, had risen to greet
them, but opposite him, sitting well back and dressed
in a dark frock, but nevertheless there in public not
ten days after the disaster, was Phillida herself.
David looked from one to the other of them. He was
white and his jaw had set.

"You *blithering* fools," he said, the old-fashioned
expletive giving the remark an emphasis which no
stronger word could have done.

"Not at all." Godolphin was brisk and even cheer-
ful. "Sit down, will you? We've something to put to
you. We were just discussing it when I happened to
see you. Very queer you should have decided to come
to just this one restaurant, isn't it?"

"I don't think it is. I probably came here for the
same reason as you did. It's not overcrowded with our
particular set. I'm sorry to speak crudely to you two,
but upon my Sam I think you're both mad."

"Sit down." Godolphin placed a chair for Frances
next to Phillida. The definite artificiality in his manner was very noticeable, and it suddenly occurred to

her that he was behaving like the amateur detective in a play. The same idea seemed to have occurred to David for he looked at him blankly.

"This is damned serious," he said at last. "You're out of touch with civilisation still, 'Dolly.' It's not what people think that matters, old boy. I don't believe that any more than you do. It's what the police may take it into their heads to consider. They've followed you both here, you know. They're bound to have. They've had a man tailing me from the beginning."

Godolphin cast an eloquent glance at Phillida and resumed his seat.

"A cigarette?" he suggested.

Frances could have screamed at him. He was slightly drunk and he was playing at it. He had come back into the midst of their genuine tragedy and was using it to gratify some idiotic theatrical sense of his own. She glanced at her half sister to see how she was taking it and was sidetracked by something else.

Phillida was wearing the chiffon which she had thrown so carelessly on one side on the night before the funeral. The smoky drapery mingled with the shadows and was hidden, but on her corsage glittered an enormous spray of diamonds. The diamond may be more often imitated than any other stone, but it is also the one least capable of disguise. The watery brilliance of the true white diamond is unmistakable, and Frances gaped at it. Phillida had a good many jewels, but a staggering effort of this sort was not a

thing one brought out lightly from a drawer in the
dressing table or even from a safe in the wall. It
seemed incredible that she should never have seen
it before.

David followed her eyes.

"That's rather sensational," he said, leaning forward. "Is it new?"

Phillida did not speak but indicated Godolphin
helplessly.

David sat back. "Yes, well, you *are* nuts," he said.
"You'll get the girl arrested, 'Dolly.' Didn't you hear
what old Mrs Ivory said? She's quite right, you know.
Look here, this isn't funny any more. I know you and
I, and Phillida too, for that matter, all belong to the
gang who grew up just after the war and found the
place in such a mess that everything had to be a
roaring joke, and we laughed ourselves along, trying
everything and feeling nothing very serious . . . as it
wasn't, then . . . but times have changed. We're old.
We're grown up. We're the ruling generation. When
we get in a mess now it's real. It's a serious mess.
You can't go assing along like this as though we were
still back in the nineteen twenties. It's disgusting as
well as being dangerous."

Godolphin cleared his throat deliberately. He was
still smiling faintly.

"I was going to talk to you tomorrow," he said,
"but we can have it out here better than anywhere
else. Frances ought to be in it too. I've been going
into this thing very thoroughly. I warned you that I
should, and I've come to some very interesting con-

clusions. Now listen to me, Field. This is straight.
You can be absolutely frank with us. We're none of us
against you. There's nothing we won't do for you,
but we must have the thing settled. Did you kill
Robert?"

David sat perfectly still, looking at them. They
could see his face had grown hard and his round dark
eyes hot with some emotion which was not defined.

"My dear chap," he said at last.

Godolphin bent forward, the energy and eagerness
in the movement reminiscent of his old form.

"That's not an answer."

David rose. Godolphin's stick lay against his chair
and he indicated it.

"When you're fit enough to do without that I'll be
happy to oblige you," he said briefly. "I take it you're
asking for horseplay?"

"Still you haven't answered me."

David appealed to Phillida. "Has he been like this
all the evening?" he began, but paused as he caught
a glimpse of her face. His colour changed and he shot
a swift enquiring glance at Frances which took her
off her guard. For a moment he stood looking at her
and his mouth twisted before he laughed. "Dear me,"
he said flippantly. "Life is full of little surprises. No,
'Dolly,' I did not kill kim."

"Yet you were the last person who could possibly
have been with him. You came out of the garden
room and told Frances that he was going for a walk.
That's common knowledge."

Godolphin's prosecuting-counsel manner was growing, and he was sprawling across the table in his eagerness.

"I did. I thought he was going out. Damn it, I'd fetched his coat and hat from the hall for him." The admission escaped him before he was aware, and he broke off abruptly before Godolphin's sharp intake of breath.

"You fetched his coat and hat?"

"Yes, I did. Don't be so damned dramatic about it. I fetched his coat and hat and chucked them on the table for him."

"Why?"

"Because he asked me to."

"Do you honestly expect anyone to believe that?"

"No. That's why I didn't mention it before. But that's what happened."

Godolphin slid back into his chair.

"Wouldn't it be easier?" he said gently. "After all, we're all on your side. We all know what Robert was and we all know you're inclined to lose your head when you lose your temper. Give us a chance to get behind you."

David leant back against the door of the box. He looked very tall in his dinner jacket. His hands were in his pockets and his head was bent.

"Why?" he said at last. "Why on God's earth *should* I have killed the chap? I admit I was having a few words with the man about my marrying Frances, but he couldn't put his foot down one way or the other. He wasn't Meyrick, and anyway the child's free, white and twenty-one."

Godolphin glanced at Phillida again as if to make sure that she was an appreciative audience.

"David," he said, "supposing you were having this backchat with Robert alone down there in the garden room, with the house quiet and the fire low, and suppose Robert said something that got under your skin. Suppose you suddenly saw him with that conceited leet on that lantern mug and his grey lock flapping in his eyes and you felt what a damned silly pompous ass he was, and you suddenly let him have it. Suppose you told him."

He broke off and they stared at David. He was white. The old friendliness had been wiped off his face as though with a sponge. Godolphin went on inexorably.

"Suppose you told him about his own wife. You knew, remember. You were the only guest at that wedding. And then, when you realised what you'd done and saw how he was going to take it, and realised that Phillida was going to be brought into it and that your marriage with Frances would be mucked up hopelessly, suppose that then you lost your head . . . as you do, you know . . . and you killed him."

"With a toothpick, I suppose?"

Godolphin shrugged his shoulders.

"There used to be an old spike file in that desk in there, so Norris says. He can't remember when it disappeared. Whatever it was you had a week to get rid of it."

David shifted his weight from the door.

"Imaginative little beggar, aren't you?" he said,

but for once his lightness did not ring true and his face was still grey.

"If you'll be reasonable I'll back you to the limit."

"David, for God's sake!" Phillida was scarcely audible.

The painter ignored them both. He looked at Frances.

"Coming?" he enquired.

She rose at once and went over to him.

"I'm sorry," said Godolphin. "You could have trusted us. I can't understand you. Don't any of you see that somebody, one of you in the house that night, must have done it? This obstinate lying is so absurd."

David put his hand on Frances' arm and took it away again.

"Coming?" he repeated.

They went out of the restaurant together in silence. The only cab available was an old one, a dreadful springless vehicle smelling like the inside of an old-clothes trunk. Frances sat bleakly in a corner of it as they jolted over the broad roads, greasy with light rain. She sat rigidly, her hands clasped between her knees, her eyes fixed on the winding vista of lamplit brilliance ahead.

They were in a traffic jam at the end of Bond Street when at last he spoke in a brittle, contemptuous tone which she had not heard before.

"And what do you think after all that?"

"I don't."

"Don't what? Think I'm guilty or think at all?"

Frances closed her eyes and her voice was dreary.

"I don't think anything except that I love you,"
she said.

He said nothing at all, and she sat there wretch-
edly, feeling that she had finished it, pulled the last
sound spar out of the whole tottering structure of life
and peace of mind. Now David was gone and that
was that.

The cab crawled on a foot or so and the light from a
standard shone directly into the little leather cabin.
A movement at her side attracted her and she turned
to find him looking at her, a fixed and horrified expression on his face.

"That's a blow below the belt, Duchess," he said.
"Do you mean it?"

"Yes," she said doggedly. "I don't even care if you
killed Robert. I don't care if you've had a dozen mis-
tresses and learnt how to be so nice to women by
falling in love with all of them. I'm not interested,
I don't mind. I'm past that."

"Darling, this is bloody dangerous." He put his
arm round her and she was surprised to find it shaking. "Don't go and do this," he said, his lips touching
her ear. "Don't, please, sweet. It hurts like stink
while it lasts and when it ends it's hell on earth. You
don't know anything about it. It's all right for me,
you see, but not for you. You're so new."

"Do you love me?"

He bent his head until his forehead rested on her
cheek.

"For my sins," he said.

After a while he drew away from her, kissing her very lightly as he raised his head and pushing her firmly away from him. He found her hand, however, and held it so tightly that he hurt her, kneading it between his own.

"I hit him," he said. "That's what happened. Lucar was there to begin with, and there was an idiotic scene in which I became insufferably upstage and refused to discuss you in front of him, and he got cheeky and Robert wouldn't or couldn't shut him up. Finally I became all theatrical and kicked the little blighter out. You heard 'Dolly' getting at me this evening over my notorious temper? That was a dig at me because I once had a row with Gabrielle down in the game room at 38. It was over Phillida, the time when she was stringing me along and running a serious affair with somebody else. This was years ago, about the time I painted your portrait. I was very much the penniless artist in those days, and Gabrielle said a few rather painful things about young men who wanted to marry money. I had an Indian club, of all things, in my hand, I remember, and there was quite a setout. I got away without doing any damage but everyone knew, or thought they knew, that I might have done some, and anyhow it all looked very bad. This affair the other night was the same sort of thing. I pitched Lucar into the passage and he went off like a streak. That was when you met him, was it? It was some little time before I came up. Tenish."

"Yes," she said huskily. "That was the time. Just after ten. He looked furious."

"Not so much as I did. Robert was livid himself, unfortunately. That was how it happened. He was still standing on the hearthrug, shaking with fury, and he said something quite unpardonable, and I hit him. I hit him very hard. In fact I barked my knuckles on his chin and cut his face badly for him. He went down like a tree, with his head on the parquet. I think I put him out for a minute or two for he lay there goggling at me and I stood looking at him for a tremendous time."

"I know. I saw you."

"Did you? Where from? The yard?"

"Yes."

"Hadn't I pulled the blind down then? No? That must have been afterwards. Yes, it was of course. I drew the blind after I'd got him into the chair and seen the mess his face was in."

He was silent for a moment or so and she heard him laugh awkwardly in the darkness.

"Such a silly, kiddish story. I was ordinarily and unintellectually angry and I seem to have behaved like an undergrad hearty, all inflammatory with first love and what not. Anyway, I remained truculent. It didn't pass. But I did have the sense to realise that I'd put up an idiotic show by marking him, and my first anxiety was to get him clean and tidy, so that his version of the story wouldn't sound too bad for anything. He was pretty worried about himself too. He kept saying, 'What will the servants think?' like a parrot, until I nearly hit him again. Finally I went out and got his hat and coat for him and told him to get into them while I went up to say good night to you. My idea was to cart him down to a doctor and get him patched up. We were going to use the yard door so that he shouldn't run the risk of meeting anyone in the hall. Well, all that was all right as far as it went, but when I came down again I heard him talking inside the room. I assumed that Lucar had returned so I didn't go in. A deep feeling of no enthusiasm for both of them descended upon me and I thought of well, what the hell. I went back down the passage, got my own coat from the cloakroom where I had left it, like an ass, when I fetched his, and let myself out. When he didn't show up in the morning I took it for granted that he was hiding somewhere, getting his face presentable."

"Why didn't you tell them all this?"

"Who? 'Dolly'?"

"No. The police."

He laughed and released her hand.

"It wouldn't have been a good idea, ducky, would it?" he said. "Lucar had brought the entire boiling down on his own head, anyway, by clearing out."

"You weren't trying to shield Lucar?"

"No, naturally not. But I saw no point in going into a long story about what he had said and what Robert had said and why I was irritated."

"In fact you were shielding me?"

He leant over and put his hands one on each side of her on the wall of the cab.

"Oh, my God, Duchess," he said heavily, "if you make a hero of me you're going to come such a howling cropper."

"I don't think I care very much about that."

He kissed her gently, almost shyly.

"I don't believe you do. Heaven help us both," he said.

13

THE DETECTIVE WAS SITTING STOLIDLY in the hall waiting for them as they came up the steps. He was apologetic. Divisional Detective Inspector Bridie, he assured them, was more than sorry to have to ask Miss Ivory to come out again at this time of night, but if she would come down to headquarters for a minute or two he would be eternally grateful.

There was not the slightest hint of compulsion in the request. It was almost abject. But the time was queer and the urgency was queer, and Frances felt again the little stab of fear under her diaphragm.

David went with them as a matter of course, and the plain-clothes man made no objection. It was an uncomfortable journey, with the two sitting stiffly in the back of a taxi and the detective silent on an occasional seat in front of them. It had begun to rain heavily again when they stumbled out across the slippery pavement, up a worn flight of steps, and crossed under the blue light into a narrow corridor neatly decorated in government green. They passed an open doorway through which they caught a glimpse of the homely charge sergeant's office, and went on up uncarpeted stairs to a waiting room which might have belonged to any railway station. There was a young constable standing by the door, and behind him, seated at the table and looking as if she was going to drop with fatigue, was Miss Dorset, of all people.

Their escort cut short any mutual greetings with a hurried apology.

"It sounds funny, I know, but I wonder if you'd mind, miss? No talking," he said. "It won't be for long. It's only regulations."

He nodded to the constable, who went off at once, leaving them all looking at one another awkwardly. Frances was openly nervous. She looked peculiarly out of place in her long white fur coat in the rigidly utilitarian surroundings. David stood close to her, dropping his hand unostentatiously over her own.

They waited for a full minute before the clatter on the boards outside announced the return of the constable. He came in ponderously, and his young eyes rested on her with open boyish admiration.

"This way, miss," he said, beaming. "The inspector was sorry to keep you waiting."

It was all very formal and old fashioned, as if the law were some elderly gentleman with a pleasant taste in servants if none in furnishings.

She left David without a glance and went with him, and afterwards, when she thought of it again, it seemed symbolic.

Bridie was sitting behind his desk, a pair of steel spectacles on the tip of his nose and no trace of weariness in his bearing. He rose when she came in and set a chair for her himself, waving the constable out of the room as he did so.

"This is a fine time to ask ye to come and see me. Did ye think ye were coming to chail?" he said cheerfully. "Would ye like a cigarette?" He indicated the ornate box on his desk but did not offer it, and seemed mildly relieved when she refused. A movement behind her made her glance round to discover a helmetless constable seated at a small desk, who was regarding her with unsmiling interest. "Ye don't want to notice him," said Bridie with terrific jocularity. "The poor chap cholly well has to sit there to take down any chewelery that may drop from ma lips."

He laughed at his own attempt at a witticism, and his eyes were human and pleased.

"Now," he said, resettling himself, "you'll probably think I'm a fussy old pairson to get ye to come down here in the middle of the night so I can ask ye something I've asked ye before, but I won't keep ye long. Ye'll be in your bed in half an hour. Would you chust repeat exactly what ye did on the night your poor dead brother-in-law . . . pardon me, half brother-in-law . . . was last seen alive?"

His friendliness, which amounted almost to gaiety, was not in the least disarming. Frances felt her scalp begin to prickle, and breathing was absurdly difficult.

"I was talking to Phillida," she said cautiously, trying to remember every word of her previous statement.

"At what time?"

"I don't know exactly. I went up at about half-past nine, I think. I'd heard the nine o'clock news on the radio. And then David arrived and he and

Robert had gone into the garden room. Robert told me not to go with them, so I went up to Phillida."

"Cholly clear," said Bridie with unnecessary enthusiasm, and the constable made a note.

Frances continued. The hideous room with its bilious walls and unshaded lights was swimming. There was no reason why she should be afraid. She had so little to hide, so little to tell, and yet her mouth was dry and her ears were singing.

"I stayed with her for some little time, about another half-hour, and then I went downstairs again as I've told you."

"So ye have, and told it well," he assured her happily. "But I'd chust like it once more. Half an hoor . . . That makes it tenish."

Tenish. David had used that ugly little word. She hesitated uncertainly. There was danger about. The smell of it was in the very air and yet she could not place it. Bridie was beaming and avuncular, and she took the plunge. After all, it was the truth. Surely there could be no harm in sticking to that?

"Yes," she said. "Just about ten. I passed Mr. Lucar in the hall and I went on down to the yard, as I said."

"Wait a minute. Ye're sure ye passed Mr Lucar at that time?"

"Yes. Perfectly sure."

"Ah," said Bridie, and the constable took another note.

"Then ye went down to the yar-rd and what did ye see?"

This was the danger point. This was the lie. She saw the real scene clearly in her mind: David alone, David standing with no expression on his face, looking down. Robert must have been lying on the floor then, goggling stupidly, the mark on his jaw slowly puffing up. It was such a little subterfuge, such a small omission. She remembered the exact words she had used before and repeated them.

"I saw David and Robert talking."

"Chust talking?"

"Yes."

"Talking," said Bridie. "Ah well, Mr Lucar will be pleased. He can sleep in his own house tonight."

He was watching her, peering out at her from under his heavy lids, and she suddenly saw the pitfall.

"Is Mr Lucar here?"

He nodded.

"Chust in there," he said, jerking his grey head towards an inner door. "He's a lucky man. For-rtunately for him there was a good conscientious woman working uncommonly late in the picture gallery that night, and she can tell how he came in for his hat and coat at ten o'clock and how they walked down to the tube together and took a train. His servant swears for him that night, and we've tr-raced his movements ever after that night ourselves. The woman gives him a grand alibi."

"Miss Dorset?"

"That's she. She's a great pairson. An honest, sensible conscientious woman, isn't she?"

The final question was shot at her, but she did not notice.

"Oh yes," she said absently, "yes, she's all right. She's absolutely cast iron. If she says it it is so. It is so," she repeated, facing the result of her little lie. David and Robert talking. David and Robert. Robert seen alive with David after Lucar was safely out of the house and in Miss Dorset's unimpeachable care. Robert never seen again.

She sat up suddenly, and Bridie pounced on her changing expression.

"What's come into your mind?"

"Nothing," she said earnestly. "Nothing."

Yet out of the whirlpool of suggestions, riddles, bewildering details and half-comprehended incidents which engulfed her something had arisen, something which set a whole procession of appalling questions racing through her mind. Since Lucar had not returned to the garden room that night David had lied to her in the taxi when he had said he had heard Robert talking to him through the door.

14

THE SOUND OF THE LATCH SLIPPING HOME
in the darkness woke Frances to full consciousness.
She sat up in bed and peered across the room, trying
to make out a deeper shadow in the black. The house
was dead. The heavy curtains over the windows shut
out all light from the street lamps and the only sound
was the faraway grumble of traffic beyond the square.

"Frances?"

The whisper started out of the silence like a fire
alarm, and she flung out her hand and caught the
tassel which turned on the bedside light. The faint
pink glow stretched out towards the door, and a
figure standing there stepped back against the portiere. It was Phillida. She was in a dark velvet wrap-
per, and above the soft plum-coloured folds her
haggard face and pale hair looked ghostly.

"What's happened?"

Frances had not meant to sound so rattled, but the
question was jerked out of her.

"Nothing else. I want to talk to you."

"Oh, I see. Very well, come over here. What time
is it?"

"Nearly four. I had to come. I couldn't stay in my

161

room another minute. Frances, you've got to listen to me. You've got to help me. I'm so frightened I don't know what to do."

"All right, of course I'll listen. Don't stand there shivering. Put the quilt round you. What is it?"

Phillida came to the end of the bed but did not sit down.

"It's 'Dolly,'" she said huskily. "If only we could get him to go away."

The younger girl eyed her curiously.

"I thought you seemed to be getting on pretty well with him tonight," she said at last.

"When he accused David? I know. That's what I mean. That's why I'm frightened. Don't you see, he's plunged into this . . . this business as if it were a new expedition or something. He's not thinking of any-one's feelings or anyone's safety. He's just fascinated by the problem. He's blind. He doesn't seem to see that it's real."

Her earnestness was disarming, even at such an hour, and Frances felt deeply sorry for her.

"Have you suggested that he went?"

"I've hinted. I didn't dare to say it outright in case it made him completely obstinate. You don't know him. He's always being like this. That was how that secret marriage happened. He forced it. He talked and bullied and got wildly and insanely enthusiastic until I simply went to pieces and let him fix it. When I saw him come limping in the other day I thought those frightful experiences out there had taken the fire out of him, but they haven't. They've rotted him up physically, but his spirit is exactly the same. What shall I do?"

Frances lay back on her pillow, with her hands behind her head, and blinked at the light.

"I don't see what you can do, darling, except bear it," she said awkwardly. "He's got all the cards. I mean you can't *turn* him out. As long as he wants to go on playing detective we shall have to let him, in view of all the circumstances."

"But, Frances, you don't understand." Phillida was still talking in whispers, but she had grown more vehement. "You don't seem to grasp what kind of person he is. Don't you realise he's been bitten by the mystery of the thing? He's seized on it and let it get hold of him. I don't believe he ever thinks of anything else, day or night. He'll go on ferreting at it until he drags the whole horrible mess out into the daylight."

"Let him." Frances passed her hands over her face. "I wish to God he would. We can't go on like this all our lives."

"Oh, but *listen*." Phillida dropped on her knees by the bedside and leant across the coverlet. "He's looking for the truth like an angry man looking for a collar stud, who wrecks everything in the room. Sometimes he gets insane ideas about things. Look how he accused David with no real evidence at all."

As Frances did not speak she leant closer.

"Frances. I haven't told this to anybody but I'm so frightened that I can't bear it any longer. He hasn't said anything direct, of course, but I can see how his mind works, and from the way he looks at

me I've wondered . . . I mean it's sneaked through
my mind . . . that . . . Oh lord, Frances, do you think
he could be so mad as to get it into his head that *I'd*
done it?"

"You? My dear girl, no. Of course not. You're off
your head. You go back to bed. You feel like this because it's nighttime. One always gets frightful ideas
in the night."

"No, it's not that. I'm not hysterical." She was
speaking with a deadly seriousness which was convincing. "Don't sound so shocked. Don't you see it's
not real to him at all? He's still living half in the
wilds. He hasn't got used to civilisation, that's all.
He thinks I might have done it."

A note in her voice startled Frances and she sat up.
"Phillida, you're not telling me that . . ."

"That I did? No, I'm not. Of course I'm not." She
dragged herself to her feet. "But there you are, you
see. Even you, you, the only person who knows I
couldn't have killed Robert, even if I'd wanted to,
you're willing to suspect me. Everyone suspects me.
The doctor does. Gabrielle does. 'Dolly' does. And
you, who know I didn't, even you're beginning to
wonder. You fool! You were with me yourself until
you went downstairs and saw Robert talking to
David. Then on your own showing you heard someone go out and after that you were hanging about the
house for a long time. You know I couldn't have done
it, could I? Could I?"

Could she? Frances found herself giving the question a consideration both levelheaded and detached.

Her own movements on the night of Robert's disappearance were stamped into her mind indelibly. She had come flying up to her own room from the yard and had stayed there until David had put his head in. A certain amount of time had elapsed between those two incidents, so there had been plenty of opportunity for Phillida to slip out of her room, hang about in one of the empty rooms downstairs, and then, when David came up . . .

Her steady train of thought leapt forward. If the person whom David had heard through the garden-room door talking to Robert had been Phillida, then not only would he not have intruded upon them, but he would never have admitted it afterwards.

Phillida leant down with her hands on the other girl's shoulders. Her face looked young and spoilt in her eagerness.

"Could I?" she repeated. "Say it. Could I?"

It was in that moment of hesitation, when the entire house seemed to be listening and the restless silence of the London night was crowding closely upon them as they huddled together in their little pool of rose-coloured light, that the thing happened.

The great brass and iron gong, which Li-Cheng, that prince of dealers, had insisted on presenting to Meyrick on the occasion of his first marriage, and which had stood in decorative opulence in a corner of the hall for thirty-five years, pitched onto the flags with a sound like all the brass instruments of creation hurling down some gigantic ravine. The things that gae bump i' the night have usually the dreadful quality of indetermination, but this was different. It was a tremendous noise and, moreover, a distinctive one. There was no possible doubt about it. Everybody in the house heard it and knew what it was.

Frances was halfway across the room, with Phillida at her heels, when the screams began. They resounded from somewhere downstairs and came, one after the other, full lunged and lusty, in a steady crescendo.

The landing was a place of fluttering half darkness when they got out there. Doors swung on their hinges and draughts fled past like live things.

"What is it? Oh, what is it? What is it?" someone was repeating shrilly, and Frances was astonished to discover that it was herself.

The reverberations of the first mighty crash still tingled in the air, and as the fifth scream died, after reaching a pitch of abandoned terror, there was a scuffle on the flags downstairs and then, for the second time in her life, Frances heard the sound which should have been so very reassuring and yet was not, the swift purposeful tread of someone marching firmly across the hall.

It was the same. That was the one thing which stood out in her mind, subduing every other thought by its significance. She choked back a cry just in time and only a deep inarticulate sound escaped her.

Phillida clutched her shoulders.

"Who is it?"

She did not answer. There was a rush of cold air and a clatter as the yard door slammed back against the wall and the screaming began again.

"For God's sake keep that blasted woman quiet! He's getting away. Stop him!"

Godolphin's voice, comfortingly human and furious, sounded in the darkness, and they heard his stick grating on the stone as he limped forward.

"Head him off by the front way. Quickly, Norris! After him! I'm following as fast as my damned leg will let me."

"All right, sir, all right." Norris' voice sounded quavery and the front door opened, letting in a blast of damp air. He shouted as he took the stone steps and Godolphin lurched after him.

Another scream, but a halfhearted one, sounded from the drawing-room door, and Frances recognised the voice.

"Mrs Sanderson!" she called, hurrying down the staircase. "Mrs Sanderson, are you hurt? I'm coming, I'm coming."

There was a theatrical gasp as she reached the hall, and a vast damp calico bundle collapsed in her arms.

"He's here," whispered the woman. "He's here again. The killer's come back."

Frances supported her. There was little else she could do if they were both not to roll on the stairs.

"Are you hurt?" she repeated.

"No, I'm not hit. He missed me."

"Then what are you screaming for? Turn the lights on." As she said them the words sounded unduly unsympathetic, but they had their effect. Mrs Sanderson drew back, startled and reproachful.

"What?"

"Turn the lights on. What are you all doing scrambling about in the dark?"

She went over to the switch by the service door and found it without difficulty. A house one has known since babyhood has few secrets, even in the dark. The candelabra sprang into a blaze, and she stood blinking in the half-light. The gong was just as she had expected to see it. It lay sprawling across its corner, a wreckage of brass dragons and wrought-iron supports, while beside her, her glistening face wearing an expression of injured amazement, was Mrs Sanderson, clearly prepared to scream again the moment the slightest cause should present itself.

"There," she whispered, flinging out a dramatic finger at nowhere in particular, "there he was."

Frances glanced past her at the open threshold through which the wind blew so freezingly. Godolphin came in almost immediately. He was wearing a plaid dressing gown, and his yellow cane looked incongruous with it, although he evidently needed it.

"The fool missed him," he said irritably. "I saw him myself, but he streaked round to the back of the square like a rabbit. Damn this leg! I had to give up. It was hopeless. He outstripped me at once." He looked down at himself regretfully and turned to greet Norris, who had come in behind him. "You're out of training," said Godolphin accusingly. "Couldn't you keep up with him?"

"No sir, I couldn't. I saw him but I couldn't catch him."

Norris, also in a dressing gown and grey with cold, looked almost as reproachful as Mrs Sanderson.

"He was gone like a flash."

"Would you know him again?"

"I wouldn't really like to say, sir. I didn't really see his face at all. It's a mite foggy and he kept into the houses at first. He was a shape in the shadows; that's all you could say."

Godolphin seemed somewhat taken aback by this rise to the dramatic possibilities of the situation, but he was still irritable.

"I don't think he got much, anyway," he said. "We were on to him too soon. Have you looked about? Anything missing?"

Norris' small eyes opened wide.

"I never thought it might be burglary, sir." He sounded relieved at the suggestion.

It was clear that Godolphin had never thought it was anything else, but now that the idea was presented to him he leapt on it.

"Good lord!" he said, adding immediately afterwards, as if it were a new thought, "Good lord! I didn't get a look at him. A man looks so different when he's running. Different height, even." He broke off and shot Frances a long, searching glance. She recognised his thought, and Phillida's observation came back to her: "It's not real to him. It fascinates him like another expedition or something."

"Did you think it was David?"

The dangerous question rose to her lips and she might have asked it had it not been for Mrs Sanderson. Until now the housekeeper had stood helpless, her hands swinging limply in front of her, while she gaped at the two men as though she did not understand them, but now she asserted herself.

"It was the nigger," she exploded. "It was the nigger come back to murder someone else."

"You hold your tongue, Mrs S.! The police told you straight to hold your tongue." Norris strode across the stones and thrust his face into her own.

"It was *him*," persisted the woman. "I can see it in your eye. You saw him. It was the nigger again." She opened her mouth, presumably to scream anew, but Norris dealt with her by placing a hand solidly across the lower half of her face.

"She's hysterical," he said, wrestling with the refractory calico bundle with an efficiency which was surprising. "She thought she saw a nigger on the day of the murder, and it's turned her blinking head. The police themselves told her to keep quiet about it. She's *advertising* herself as unbalanced, that's what she's doing. Keep quiet, Mrs S., do."

A masterly jab in the stomach from the housekeeper's elbow silenced him with a squeak, and the good lady emerged from his arms dishevelled and furious.

"You leave me be!" she exploded. "I did see him and the police complimented me on the clear way I told it. I saw him all right, and Molly saw him, and where is she now? Dead in 'er bed very likely. He's been back to take 'is toll."

"Highly improbable." The thin voice from the top

of the stairs silenced everybody. The old Gabrielle stood there, dripping with lace shawls and resting on Dorothea's arm. Phillida was a step or two behind her, and together they made a dramatic group.

"Where is the girl?" Gabrielle addressed the house at large and was answered.

"Here, ma'am." A scrubby object, all loose hairs and cheap negligee, wriggled self-consciously out of the drawing-room door and wavered in the centre of the stage.

"How long have you been hiding there?" Gabrielle was in her more omnipotent mood.

"Since we heard the moving about, ma'am."

"When was that?"

"Just before the gong fell over, ma'am."

"My God," said Gabrielle conversationally. "My God, what next? You, Mr Godolphin, what are you doing running about the house dressed up like that?"

The admonitory tone, the implied insult to his dressing gown and her tremendous advantage of position combined to bring Godolphin to attention and to take the wind out of his sails at one sweeping blow. He straightened himself and coloured but he answered pertinently enough.

"I heard the door that leads into the yard open and close and I came down to investigate. On the way I ran into Norris, who had heard the same thing. In the hall here we surprised somebody who made a dash for it and knocked over the gong. Then Mrs Sanderson began to scream, and the fellow, whoever he was, got away."

Gabrielle turned to look at Phillida.

"When I was mistress of this house I had it locked at night," she said acidly. "It saved a lot of inconvenience."

"But the door was locked, ma'am. I did it myself." Norris was almost in tears. "That's why I was so took aback. Whoever came in must have had a second key."

"Impossible." Gabrielle spoke flatly, almost carelessly. "Did anybody see this burglar?"

"We're wondering if it was a burglar, darling." Frances felt her voice was unnecessarily low.

"Are you, my dear? Did anybody see him?"

"Both Norris and I caught a glimpse of the man, Mrs Ivory." Godolphin was recovering his authority. "It was very foggy outside, and he went off like a hare. We just saw him for a moment, that was all."

"And was he a Negro?"

The enquiry, coming from her in all seriousness, was astonishing, and they gaped at her. Godolphin looked at Norris, who seemed bewildered.

"No," he said. "No, ma'am. That is, I don't think so. Do you, sir?"

"No, I don't," said Godolphin dubiously. "One can't be certain, of course, but it wasn't my impression."

"Ah," said Gabrielle as if she had established an important point. "And if it wasn't burglary why do you suppose this person came?"

"To fetch the weapon," said Mrs Sanderson, and the simplicity of the statement was impressive. "As

soon as I heard someone creeping about in the house
it came to me. No one's found the weapon. The police
have searched for it high and low but they didn't
know where to look. He knew where to look and he's
come back for it. He must have had a minute or two
in the house before Mr Godolphin and Mr Norris
surprised him. He's gone straight to the spot and
got it."

They humoured her, or flattered themselves that
they did, while they satisfied their own natural
curiosity. All the downstairs rooms save one presented the placid vacant look which daytime cham-
bers always have when startled into life in the middle
of the night. The last room they searched was the
garden room, and there the change was slight but
very disturbing in the circumstances. In that cold
room which a few hours before had been left as
severely neat as a nun's cubicle a chair had been
drawn up to the table, while behind it the door of the
cupboard, which had been closed ever since the last
police expert had examined it, hung swinging open,
exposing a hungry emptiness.

Godolphin, who had led the exploring party,
stepped back abruptly, and Phillida caught her
breath audibly. Mrs Sanderson thrust her way
through the group and stood looking at the ordinary
and yet in the circumstances singularly sinister scene.

"There you are," she said. "What did I say? It was
the murderer. He's been back for the weapon, and
you know what that means . . . He's going to use it
again."

The crude melodrama of the statement would have struck most of them as ludicrous on an ordinary occasion, but that night, in the bare room before the gaping cupboard, the lurid words in the shrill north-country voice were not humorous at all.

15

IN THE MORNING, WHEN THE POLICE HAD
been informed and were still wandering round the
house with that ostentatious effort at self-effacement
which is guaranteed to fray the strongest nerves,
when David had called to see Gabrielle and had spent
an hour with her, and when Godolphin had disorgan-
ised what was left of the normal domestic routine by
taking every servant in the house over and over every
incident in the night's adventure, Lucar delivered his
invitation.

There is something about real impudence which is
a force in itself, and the terse notes which arrived
from him for every member of the family, stating
fully in the most abominable of commercial English
that he would be glad if they would give him their
attention for half an hour at three o'clock in Meyrick's office at the gallery, had the quality of an
ultimatum.

To their own and each other's astonishment they
went meekly. It was an extraordinary gathering.
Everyone was quiet and everyone was angry. As
Frances looked round her and saw Phillida, waxy and
hollow eyed, sitting sullen in her furs, Godolphin
trembling with suppressed irritation and fidgeting

with his stick as if he would like to use it, David aloof and for once completely removed from her, Miss Dorset red eyed and shocked into outraged silence, and Lucar odiously pleased with himself behind Meyrick's second desk, the fact which had been scratching at the back of her mind for the past week came home to her abruptly. No one really trusted anyone else any more. Each person in that unhappy group, all tied together by every known bond of blood or affection, and who were isolated by a sea of scandal and suspicion from the rest of their kind, had at one time or another during the last few days secretly suspected each of the rest in turn of the one crime which is never forgiven in a civilised community, the one social sin which everyone still takes seriously.

Lucar looked round with a brief smile. That derisive grin seemed to escape him by accident, for he controlled it instantly, but they had all seen it and had all found it disturbing.

"I don't see the old lady yet," he said. "We want her."

They gaped at him and he enjoyed their astonishment.

"She'll come," he remarked.

David stirred. "What are you going to do, Lucar? Confess?"

The drawling question was intentionally offensive, and they had the satisfaction of seeing the man redden. However, he kept his temper and eyed the other man from beneath his thick lids.

"That would suit you, wouldn't it?" he said.

"You've been watching me, Mr Godolphin. Placed me yet?"

The sarcasm seemed to be lost on Godolphin.

"Yes," he said. "You were Robert Madrigal's bat-man. An inefficient servant."

Frances got up. "This is silly," she said, her voice sounding unexpectedly authoritative in the electric silence. "It's no good sitting round here and insulting one another. What do you want to say, Mr Lucar? You've asked us to meet you and here we are. In a way it's extraordinary that we should have come. The fact that we have shows that we're all pretty near the end of our resources, so now you've got us here do say what you've got to say, for heaven's sake."

Lucar turned to her. "That's not quite the line to take with me," he began.

"My proud beauty," supplemented David under his breath.

Lucar swung towards him savagely.

"That'll do from you. That'll do from the lot of you. I've got you and you know it, but I'm going to put the position to you so clearly that you can't make any mistake. I'm only waiting for Mrs Ivory."

"In that case we may as well go home." Frances spoke wearily. The whole thing was slipping out of gear. "Oh, come down to earth," she said. "Is Granny likely to come all the way up here just because you've asked her to? Can't you see it's a miracle we've come ourselves? It's only because we don't know where to turn and we're clutching at straws. I'm sorry to be so forthright, but it's about time somebody said something out straight. It seems to me that you're so pleased that you're not arrested that it's turned your head. Of course Granny won't come to you. It's cheek of you to ask her, appalling cheek."

She paused. Lucar was smirking and David came over to her.

"Hold it, Duchess," he murmured and pulled her round to face the door.

Gabrielle was making an entrance. On her way down the passage she had been leaning on Dorothea's arm, but now she came forward alone, looking like some great old actress arriving to present the prizes. She was in full mourning, made almost bulky by a fox cape hanging to her knees and surmounted, most unexpectedly, but very charmingly, by an old-fashioned widow's cap with a starched and goffered lining and a long dark veil hanging down behind. Her natural dignity saved the situation, and even in the midst of his triumph Lucar evidently felt that she had somehow scored over him.

She sat down in the armchair, and Dorothea, looking very solid and respectable in her black, planted herself at her elbow.

It was at this point that the wind rose again or, to be exact, that the little company first noticed it. The long brocade curtains behind Lucar billowed out as a great gust came rushing through the narrow slit at the top of the tall window. Miss Dorset sprang to close the sash but not before a pile of flimsy papers had been strewn over the floor and Phillida had exclaimed with nervous spitefulness at the interruption.

It was typical of the afternoon that this trivial incident should have impressed itself so vividly upon their minds, and to the end of her days Frances was to feel a twinge of apprehension whenever a curtain should swing out suddenly in the rising wind.

It was Godolphin who opened the ball, sitting forward on his hard chair, his folded hands resting on the crook of his stick. After his first thrust he had been quietly superior, listening to Frances' outburst with the weariness of the expert with the child, but now he spoke practically.

"Now," he said, "now, my man, perhaps you'll explain yourself. What the devil did you mean by cutting and running the moment poor Madrigal was found dead? Didn't you realise you'd have the police after you like a pack of hounds?"

Lucar looked up from the desk where he sat in Meyrick's chair, drawing circles with Meyrick's pen on Meyrick's blotter. He was glistening with conceit.

"Not very politely asked," he said primly, "but I'll answer you. I went before I knew he was dead. Anyone can tell you that. The police saw that at once when I pointed it out to them. What I did was very simple. On the night before the discovery I happened to hear that a certain collector in London was interested in the Gaylord Venus. That information came into this office, and I saw an opportunity of doing myself a bit of good. Madrigal was out of the way. I couldn't find him to ask his opinion even if I wanted to. So I slept the night on it and decided to take the affair into my own hands. I went down to the bank and drew out all the cash I had and nipped on a boat for New York. I didn't tell a soul because the fewer people you tell when it's a question of a deal of this sort the better. I reckoned that if anyone could make Damon Penryth of Philadelphia sell that picture it was little Henry. In mid-ocean the news about Madrigal came through on the radio. I put two and two together and decided to come back. I sent a wire to the police at once, and they met me off the boat. We soon understood one another. I was all right. I knew that all along."

"That was why you came back, of course?"

Lucar lowered one thick white eyelid.

"Partly," he said.

"I don't see why you had to take your own money, Mr Lucar."

The observation was forced out of Miss Dorset by sheer indignation. "That was ordinary routine intelligence and our property."

"Never mind." Gabrielle's distaste was a Victorian tour de force. "I imagine that Mr Lucar . . . is it . . . did not ask us here to discuss a piece of very ordinary business chicanery on his part. What have you got to tell us, Mr Lucar, that you feel we might find interesting?" She was quite insufferable and meant to be. They all were. They all sat round, hating him, despising him for his vulgarity and his pettiness, and yet they hung on his words. It was very alarming.

Lucar appeared to be enjoying himself.

"Well, you know," he said softly, "I thought we all ought to have a little chat. You see, I've got my position to think of. The guv'nor's coming back, isn't he? And I may decide to stay with the firm."

They watched him blankly. After all, as Gabrielle remarked afterwards, there is nothing actually unbelievable about mass blackmail, but it is so very unconventional that it startles one.

"I don't think we understand you, Lucar."

It was David, sounding dangerously quiet.

"That's a pity, Field." Lucar shot the words out with unexpected savagery. "I rather hoped you would . . . you particularly."

"I'm afraid I don't, all the same."

"Oh, you don't? Then I'll tell you. You're in a jam, aren't you? All of you. While I was out of the country there was always a chance, from the point of view of the people who didn't know, that I was the person the police were after. My absence seemed to let you out. It didn't really. Anyone who was close to the business saw that. But to the man in the street I was a good enough scapegoat. However, now I'm back, now I've had my little talk with the police and they've shown that they're not interested in me, all that's altered. Now do you see where I'm leading?"

Nobody answered him, and his smile grew more pronounced.

"You're leaving me to do all the talking, aren't you?" he said. "I don't care. If you want it put in words you can have it. It's all the same to me. My freedom puts a rope round you. Don't you kid your-

selves it isn't there. Don't you imagine the police are
going to sleep. There's a lot of work being done on
the quiet. A lot of little odds and ends of information
are finding their way onto the superintendent's desk.
But so far they haven't had all my contribution."

"You're suggesting that we don't want the police
to find Robert's murderer," said Frances abruptly.

He turned towards her.

"One of you doesn't," he said, "and none of you
will."

"What the hell are you saying?" Godolphin rose
painfully to his feet. "We've listened to quite enough
of this," he said. "This is the kind of thing one might
have expected from you, Lucar. You were a snivelling
little nuisance on the last occasion I had anything to
do with you. I remember you, always whining and
sneaking food. When I went off to do my damned silly
heroics I looked down at you sleeping by Madrigal's
feet and I thought then it was a wasted effort."

The force of his contempt was tremendous, and
they glanced at him slyly out of the corners of their
eyes. Great heroism, like great cowardice, is shy-
making, and they were all, in spite of their other
emotions crowding upon them, embarrassed when he
mentioned the story which had made headlines when
Robert Madrigal had returned to civilisation to tell it.

Lucar met Godolphin's eyes for a moment and
flushed as he looked away.

"All right, say what you like," he said doggedly.
"Think what you like. I don't care. I've never cared
what anyone said or thought about me and that's

how I've got where I am. I know what I want and I
go for it, and if any of you has any sense at all you'll
keep quiet and you'll keep civil. One of you here
killed Madrigal. If that's not clear to you believe me
it is to the rest of the world. In your hearts you know
it. That's why you're here. That's why you're listening. Well, now you know where you stand. So far
I'm not telling any more of what I know than is
necessary to clear myself, and if everything goes on
as I intend it shall I shan't feel called upon to say
any more. I thought I'd tell you all and I'd tell you
all together, so no one makes any mistakes."

Godolphin limped to the desk and picked up the
telephone.

"Put me on to the police," he said briefly into the
instrument.

Lucar leant forward and laid a finger on the stand,
destroying the connection.

"Wait," he said. "You're not the only pebble on
the beach, Godolphin. Let the others have a say.
There are enough witnesses here to make the police
give me a gruelling, but does everybody here *want*
me to talk?"

There was a freezing silence. Godolphin stood with
the instrument still raised, and Lucar kept his finger
on the stand.

"Well," he said, "now's your opportunity."

"No." It was Gabrielle. Her voice was almost
harsh. "No," she said again. "Sit down, Mr Godolphin. When the time comes we will call the police."

There were at least three sighs in the room, and a

splatter of rain swept the window in that long moment wherein Godolphin replaced the telephone and Lucar smiled again.

"Someone's seen the light," he said and nodded to Gabrielle as no one had ever nodded to her in nearly ninety years.

"It's bluff," said David, clearing his throat. "Pure bluff. There's no earthly reason why the thing shouldn't have been done from outside."

"Isn't there?" Lucar's mouth twisted with grim amusement. "Isn't there any reason why whoever killed Madrigal could disappear quietly out of that dark house over there when the first person who goes in without knowing the place raises half the servants and kicks over a gong the moment he sets foot in it?"

Frances received a mental thump between the shoulder blades. That was the thing. That was the unformed question which had been worrying her from the beginning. That was the thing which had been wrong. Those quick, firm footsteps marching so surely across the hall, once last night and once on that other night nearly a fortnight before; they had sounded in the dark. They had crossed the dark hall where the gong stood and where there might have been a dozen other obstacles. Whoever owned those footsteps had been peculiarly sure of the ground.

She caught sight of Gabrielle and Dorothea. The two old women were regarding the redheaded man behind the desk as if he were an apparition. They knew the house, of course. For thirty years they had known every inch of it. But that idea was so pre-

posterous that Frances smiled and did not see David
glance so nervously at Phillida.

Lucar seemed satisfied with the impression he was
making. He leant back in Meyrick's chair and crossed
his plump legs.

"The police seem to be taking a lot of interest in a
nigger some scivvy thought she saw," he remarked.
"I didn't give my opinion on that idea because I
wasn't asked for it. I'm much more interested in
certain other little things . . . the music-hall song, for
instance."

He regarded their stony faces with growing satisfaction.

"No one really amused?" he said. "That's a funny
thing. It's a famous old song. 'No one's going to kiss
that girl but me.' You know how it goes. 'Pride of
Idaho, So now you know If you go You'll find there's
something on her mind Don't think it's you, Cause
no one's going to kiss that girl but me.' Don't you
get it, anybody? Let me whistle it to you."

He pursed his lips, and the catchy tune sounded
shrill and clear in the crowded room. It was not quite
an errand boy's version; now was it strictly correct.
There was an individuality about it and an element
of great weariness.

"Oh, my God," said Miss Dorset, her voice thick
and deep in her throat. "The whistle on the telephone."

"Was that it?" Phillida and Gabrielle spoke together and both broke off in the same way as if they
had said too much.

"What's this? I haven't been told about this."
Godolphin turned towards them eagerly, all his anger
evaporating before his interest in the new clue.

"You recognise it, do you?" Lucar was watching
Miss Dorset with his head on one side.

"Yes, I heard it ... once." The woman spoke dully.
She was frightened. Fear showed in her heavy eyes
and in the way her mouth quavered. "It was about
eight months ... ten ... no, nearly a year ago. A call
came through for Mr Madrigal here at the office.
I didn't recognise the voice. It was foreign and sort of
constrained. Something about it made me curious,
and I listened for a moment or two. That was all I
heard, just the tune whistled like that. Then Mr
Madrigal hung up. He went out at once and didn't
come back all day."

She paused.

"I never saw him quite the same after that," she
added presently.

Godolphin was looking at her as if he thought she
was gibbering.

"That doesn't sound like you," he said. "I mean
that's a fantastic story. It's melodrama. It sounds
like the fakir's curse. Pull yourself together. What
really happened?"

"It's true." Phillida was sitting bolt upright, two
spots of colour burning in her cheeks. "It often happened, or at least he thought it did. It became an
obsession with him. He used to dream about it.
That's what frightened me so. I thought he was out
of his mind. That day after—after we found him I

told Gabrielle up in the bedroom and she thought I
was mad. Now Miss Dorset's telling you, and you're
looking at her as if she . . ."

The words died, and a trickle of laughter escaped
her, growing in volume and rising high and uncon-
trolled. Gabrielle moved with surprising agility.

"Quick," she said, "quick, somebody."

It was Frances who reached her first and who shook
the hysteria out of her.

"All right," said Godolphin when the excitement
had died a little. "All right, all right. There's no need
to go off the deep end about it, Phillida. If you all
say it did happen I'll accept it. I knew Robert pretty
well, though, and I can't say I see him as a nervous
wreck. Are you sure he wasn't pulling your leg?"

"Oh no, you're on the wrong tack there entirely.
Robert had changed. Last time I saw him that's exactly how I should have described him, a nervous
wreck."

David made the statement quietly, almost casually, and his expression did not change before Godolphin's incredulous stare.

"I heard it once," said Miss Dorset again. "As I
told you, I heard it once, but I always knew when it
happened by the way he behaved."

"Amazing," said Godolphin. "I believe you, of
course, but it is amazing, isn't it? How often did this
occur? Once a month? Once a week?"

"Pretty regularly at the finish, wasn't it?" Lucar
put the question to the woman slyly, as if they shared
a confidence. "It began about a year ago, and it's

been happening at irregular intervals ever since. Isn't
that your impression, Mrs Madrigal?"

Phillida covered her face with her hands.

"Yes, I think so." Her voice was smothered. "He
was getting more and more on edge all the time. It
was only since the summer that he began to talk so
wildly about it, and I began to think he was insane."

"There's nothing insane about it if Miss Dorset
heard it too," Godolphin declared practically.

"Exactly. That's my point," Lucar's tone was
quiet, but it brought them all round facing him again.
"Well, there you are," he said. "That's all I'm telling
at the moment, but I've got a hunch it's going to be
enough. You can ring up the police if you like, but all
I say is before any one of you does so I'd make sure
your best friend wants you to. Now I won't detain
you. I dare say you'll all feel like a little discussion
without me. I'm sorry I can't offer you this room but
I'm going to be busy. However, the rest of the
mausoleum is at your disposal. Miss Dorset, I'll have
a cup of tea in here at four-fifteen."

It was the final insult, the last twist of the screw,
and he looked round him eagerly to see if his hold
was secure.

On the other side of the room Frances also looked
about her. She was waiting for the outcry, the single
annihilating stroke which would send him back where
he belonged. It did not come. They were going to
stomach it. The realisation came to her with a sense
of dismay. It was unbelievable but also obvious.

Gabrielle had lain a restraining hand on Godolphin's sleeve, and the rest were silent and expressionless.

They went, leaving Lucar in his triumph, and trooped into the antique room. It was deserted, and there was an awkward pause as Gabrielle, who had headed the procession of defeat, leaning on Dorothea for support, paused and faced her flock.

"I shall sit here," she announced, fixing Miss Dorset with eyes which were still bright in spite of her weariness. "Tell them to keep the public out of here. This gallery is closed."

"Darling, do you think you ought to?" It was not like Phillida to be solicitous, but she sounded sincere. "You ought to go to bed after all that. I shall myself. I can't stand it. I can't stand it any longer."

Gabrielle beckoned Godolphin.

"Take her home," she said. "All of you go out of here. Do you mind? I want to be alone except for Dorothea. I am old, too old. I want to sit here and rest and make up my mind."

There was nothing to be said after that. She had issued orders for nearly eighty years and had acquired an art in the matter.

The rest of them moved out onto the staircase and stood about in two little groups, whispering. David paused by Frances.

"I'm going back to the studio," he said abruptly. "I've got some work."

"To work?" It was an unexpected announcement at such a time and she echoed him.

He nodded. "Yes. I've got a drawing, a portrait, I must finish. I'll see you soon. Stay in for me this evening. I'll ring you."

She said nothing and he laughed and, taking one of her hands, squeezed it violently before he turned away and hurried off down the stairs, leaving her looking after him.

Frances moved to the long landing window and knelt up on the low sill, to look down into the square and see him go. It was nearly dusk and the lamps were yellow in the blue haze. She could not see the house next door because of the corner, but the square was there with the blackened trees swinging in the wind and the passers-by walking with their heads down, clutching their hats, while their coat skirts clung to them cripplingly or floated out like banners. There was no sign of David, and she took it that she had missed him. All the same she did not move. The familiar scene outside was peaceful and normal at a moment when ordinary reflection was impossible. At that time her mind was a confused dumping ground of fears and impressions, and she was grateful for a moment's respite. For a while she behaved like a child, counting the familiar railings, watching the taxicabs and the sleek private cars, forcing her newest terrors with the old ones far back behind her consciousness and living resolutely in the immediate present.

She did not notice the others go, nor did she see the various employees who passed her. She remained staring out of the window for nearly twenty minutes, simply kneeling upon the sill, contemplating the traffic.

It was the hullabaloo at the back of the building which recalled her to the present. The clatter of the restaurant tray on the parquet was the first alarm, and the babel followed when the office boy shouted the news.

It had been four-fifteen exactly when that young man knocked on the door of Meyrick's room and carried in the tea which Lucar had ordered so ungraciously. He had been halfway to the desk when he had seen the man and the tray had slipped from his hand.

Lucar was dead. Even a fourteen-year-old office teamaker had seen that much. The smug expression was still on his face, and he still sat in Meyrick's chair, but there was a narrow wound in his side where a thin steel blade had slid in between his ribs, piercing the chest wall and penetrating the heart itself. Lucar had died as Robert Madrigal had died, instantly and without a sound, and once again there was no trace of any weapon.

It was while the entire staff of the gallery was crowding on the back staircase, the only approach to the office while Gabrielle remained in possession of the antique room, that Frances, still not fully conscious of the smothered uproar two walls behind her, suddenly saw David Field come down the steps directly under the window and hurry off across the road.

16

AT EIGHT O'CLOCK THERE WERE STILL
lights in the gallery, while in the house next door
there was that atmosphere of bustle which alone
makes crises bearable. As Frances carried two hot-
water bottles across the hall she hardly noticed the
plain-clothes man, sitting there silent and official.
She hurried up the stairs for the twentieth time since
Phillida's condition had become acute without looking at him. She had grown used to him, and his rigor-
ously noncommittal attitude was no longer even
alarming.

Godolphin remained exactly where she had left
him. He was still leaning over the banisters on the
landing, his arm folded on the rail where the doctor's
coat hung, and he did not glance at her as she passed.

The upper hall looked strange with all the doors
open, and glimpses of the lighted rooms within were
intimate and homely. Blankets lay about in piles
and the linen press stood open, while the trolley
bearing basins and ewers, which was drawn up outside the sickroom, added to the general air of desha-
bille. 38 Sallet Square was no longer a grande dame
but a lady in her petticoat with her stockings coming
down. There were whispers everywhere, the rattling

of crocks and the hissing of kettles, hurrying footsteps and doors closing quietly.

Mrs Sanderson, who wore a great white apron to
impress the doctor with her efficiency, came tiptoeing
out of Phillida's room with two bundles in her arms.

"I'm just going to heat these bricks up again," she
murmured as they met. "When it comes to warmth
you can't beat a brick. Just go in, miss. Don't knock.
Poor thing, she's delirious again. Can you wonder at
it? It's a miracle to me we're not all crawling up the
walls. Norris has been sick twice himself. That's pure
nerves. They affect the stomach in some people."

She sped on and crackled starchily down the stairs
while Frances let herself into Phillida's bedroom.

It was very warm in there, and old Dorothea bent
over the fire where a small brass kettle was boiling.
The doctor was standing at the end of the bed, his
hands clasped loosely behind him. Frances was tremendously grateful to him. He was friendly enough
but he also possessed, in manner at any rate, that
superb quality of superhumanity which made it seem
safe for Phillida to toss and mutter as much as she
liked.

Dorothea took the bottles and put them in the bed.
She was muttering to herself all the time and sniffing
most irritatingly, but all her movements were strong
and cobby, which made her seem the embodiment of
capability itself.

"Poor thing," she was saying in a monotonous
undertone. "Poor thing. Tch, tch, tch! Poor thing.
Poor silly thing."

Phillida lay with her lids parted, the narrow slits showing far too much of the whites of the eyeballs. She might have been an old woman, her face shrunken, with the nose pinched and the lips grey. Every now and again she spoke in a drunken whisper. It was for the most part indistinguishable, but single words came out with startling clarity.

"Daydream," said Dorothea. "She keeps saying 'daydream.' No warmth. No warmth yet. It's not right. Her hand's like a stone."

The doctor took Phillida's pulse again. He made no comment but replaced the limp arm very carefully and tucked the covers well over it.

"What's she done?" Frances put the question abruptly. "That can't be just fright, can it?"

"Shock?" he said, smiling faintly at her. "Oh, can't it! She's had the equivalent of a kick over the heart. If you think of it like that it makes it much more comprehensible. There's nothing like emotion to upset the circulatory system. She was in a bad nervous condition to begin with, and this last shock seems to have toppled her over the edge."

"Will she be all right?"

He did not answer immediately but turned back to the bed.

"I think so," he said at last. "The only real danger at the moment is from infection. In a state like this resistance is practically nil, so there's always a danger from pneumonia or any other bug there may be about. She'll need constant watching."

Frances did not understand the dubious note in the last few words.

"You mean she can't be moved to a nursing home? Of course not. But can't we have a couple of good nurses here? It's a big house and there are plenty of bedrooms."

He hesitated, looking very uncomfortable.

"That would be ideal, of course, if it could be arranged."

"Well, can't it? Can't you telephone and get someone?"

"I could try," he agreed slowly, and she suddenly saw his difficulty and turned a little white.

"You mean they might not care to come to us?" The dismay on the small heart-shaped face turned up to him was so frank that he patted her shoulder.

"Well, it's an awkward time, isn't it?" he said gently. "It's no good having anyone second rate, either. Still, I'll try. I know the Pelham Street people pretty well, well enough to put it all to them. I'll see what I can do. I don't think I'll use this phone."

"No, no, of course not." Frances felt unsteady on her feet. Nothing else had brought the situation home to her quite so clearly. "There's an extension in my room next door. Will you come?"

She led him to it and was going out again when he stopped her.

"I wonder if you'd mind?" he said. "Just a minute. I'd like a few words with you if I may. Perhaps we'd better have the door closed. Mrs Madrigal's collapse occurred immediately after she heard the news of Mr Lucar's death, did it? Who told her? You?"

"I'm afraid I did. I helped Dorothea to bring my grandmother over from the gallery and then I went in to see Phillida. She was just going to bed. She had felt groggy all day, and I ought to have had more sense than to blurt the whole thing out. But I'm afraid I've grown so used to Phillida being ill. We all have."

He nodded gravely. "Naturally," he said. "There's so little to show in these nervous conditions. You simply told her flatly, did you?"

"I said Lucar had been killed."

"And then she collapsed?"

"Yes. I thought she'd merely fainted. I called Dorothea and we got her on the bed. Then I saw that her forehead was wet and we realised how cold she was. That was when I got on to you."

"I see," he said but he still hesitated, and she struggled on with her explanations. It seemed desperately important that everything should be made very clear, yet every word seemed to make things a little worse.

"We'd been having a sort of family conference," she volunteered. "Mr Lucar called it himself in my father's office in the gallery next door. When it was over most of us stayed there for a bit, in the building, I mean, but Phillida felt rotten, so Mr Godolphin brought her back here at once."

"Oh, did he?" The doctor brightened. "I hadn't

realised that. Did he stay with her until you came?"

"No." Frances paused uncertainly. It was very difficult. Even to see his inference would be dangerous. "No," she repeated presently, "he didn't, as a matter of fact. He had to go out in a car."

"In a car?"

"Yes. I'm so sorry I'm being vague. It's quite simple really. You see, as they came back they saw the new car which Godolphin is thinking of buying had been sent along by the showroom people. The salesman had been waiting for some time, so Godolphin merely planted Phillida in her room and went off down again to try the car."

"Then she was alone in the house for . . . say . . . a half to three quarters of an hour before you came?"

"About half an hour. Lucar was found twenty minutes after we'd all left him, and we came over here almost immediately we heard what had happened. Because of Granny, you see. The servants were here all the time, of course."

"But weren't they in the basement?"

"They may have been. In fact, yes, they probably were most of the time."

"I see," he said again and stood looking at her, his tired face flushed with embarrassment. She was not looking very happy herself, and the shadows under her eyes were alarming. He smiled at her wryly. "You'll have to take it carefully yourself," he said. "It's an appalling ordeal. Look here, this isn't quite ordinary inquisitiveness, but there is one point I would like to know. Is there any connecting door between this house and the gallery?"

Frances flushed. The bright colour flowed over her face and neck, making her look younger than ever.

"Yes," she said reluctantly. "It's Meyrick's own door. That's my father, of course. No one else ever dreams of using it. That's why it never occurred to any of us to go that way this afternoon, although if would have been much more sensible for Gabrielle. It may sound queer to you, but I've never been through that door in my life. Meyrick made a fetish of it."

"Where is it?"

She took a deep breath. After all, what did it matter? The police knew now and tomorrow everyone else would know.

"It opens from the back of the cupboard in Meyrick's bedroom," she said slowly, "and it leads into his office."

"His office? Isn't that where Mr Lucar died?"

She nodded miserably and he was acutely sorry for her, but he was also curious.

"If it wasn't used by anyone except your father I suppose it was kept locked?"

Frances shrugged her shoulders. She had expected this from the police, but if it had to come from the doctor what, after all, did it matter?

"It was bolted from this side," she said. "Meyrick kept it like that except when he was actually in the gallery, and when he went away it was left bolted. My grandmother has that bedroom now, and the

connecting door was still bolted when we came back
this afternoon. She's hardly ever out of the room,
you see."

"Yet she was when Mr Lucar was killed?"

"Yes. She was over in the gallery."

He glanced at the telephone. "It's all extremely
awkward," he said. "You realise that in all fairness I
should have to explain the situation to any nurse
who came?"

"For God's sake get someone discreet." The words
were out of her mouth before she could stop them.

He glanced up sharply, and for a moment they
eyed one another.

"Yes," he said, "that's important too. Well, I'll
see. I can't promise but I'll see."

She left him dialling the number and was about to
return to the sickroom when she saw Mrs Sanderson
as she came out on the landing. Godolphin had disappeared from his sentry post, and she thought she
heard him whispering to Dorothea round the corner
by the sickroom door. Mrs Sanderson was evidently
lying in wait for her. She was halfway up the staircase
and now stood beckoning, conveying both haste and
caution by a great deal of elaborate dumb show.

As Frances came forward so she retreated, leading
her across the hall to the breakfast room with such
ostentatious nonchalance that the plain-clothes man
regarded them both hopefully. However, once in
safety, with the door shut firmly behind them, her
manner underwent a startling change.

"You must sit down, miss," she said, leering at her

with cow-eyed pity at least three parts genuine. "Sit down and get out your handkerchief. I've just heard something that I think you ought to know before anyone else. Be brave, my dear. They've got him."

It worked. Frances was never quite able to forgive Mrs Sanderson or herself for that. A sinking void seemed to heave and swallow her and the brightly lit familiar room grew dark. She was aware first of her own hands gripping the table ledge so tightly that the wood hurt her fingers. The other woman watched her, compassion mixed with open satisfaction. She was a ghoul by temperament but not an unkindly one.

"Molly got it out of the man on the back door," she said. "They found his address and sent and took him down to the station. There's been no end of goings on at the gallery," she added, not without a touch of wistfulness. "Poor Mr David! You won't believe it, will you?"

The last question was an entreaty, not to say a threat, and in spite of everything it struck Frances as funny. At the same time it occurred to her that it would strike David as being even funnier, and the picture of his personality which the thought conjured up brought her to her senses.

"No," she said with a brisk conviction which almost spoiled Mrs Sanderson's moment, it sounded so authoritative. "No, of course not."

"He's at the station," persisted the housekeeper, making it clear that she hoped for gallantry rather than optimism. "Of course everybody knows now what happened. Mr Lucar told his suspicions, and the murderer 'ad to strike again. It's very terrible. He was such a nice man. I never should 'ave believed 'e would 'ave done it. Still, you never can tell. Every 'uman 'ead is a mystery bag, that's what I say. Now you'll want to go away and have a good cry, won't you? There's no one in the servants' hall. You'd never be disturbed there. I'll make you a hot malted milk."

"No, I must go back to Phillida," said Frances, feeling more and more like the boy on the burning deck, yet assailed by an idiotic inclination to accept the offer.

"My brave girl!" There were real tears in Mrs Sanderson's eyes. Frances fled.

The plain-clothes man was not at his post, and it did not occur to her until afterwards that he had gone into the drawing room to listen through the inner door to the housekeeper's revelations. Just at that moment very few things were clear to her. It was not a time for intelligent thinking. David arrested? David proved guilty? David proved to have killed Robert, and afterwards Lucar? It was absurd, ridiculous, impossible, not likely to be true, out of character, insane.

Insane? The word burst in her mind like a flare, lighting up odd corners of her memory with a vivid and unnatural light. To most people insanity is a dreadful mystery, a werewolf of a thing. More fantastic beliefs are held by the layman about insanity than about anything else in the civilised world. Frances was no alienist. She too had been brought up to believe in the shibboleths, and the smiling, mild-mannered homicidal maniac of superhuman strength and agility was a reality to her.

Insanity. The word opened up a dozen possibilities. Closed doors were thrown wide, showing dark, ugly vistas within. If someone near and close should prove to be insane then anything was possible.

She had reached the foot of the stairs and had paused there, trying to get a hold on herself, when some way behind her, round the angle of the passage, out of sight yet near, the door of the garden room closed softly.

She stood listening. It was dark down that corridor, yet whoever was walking there did not trouble to turn on the light. She heard the footsteps on the stones, confident and yet careful. She had only a few seconds to wait. Nearer came the patter on the marble, nearer and nearer.

And then, as at last a figure emerged, she swung round, astonishment ousting all other emotions.

It was Gabrielle. She was quite alone and she looked unexpectedly commanding in a fitted quilted dressing gown made like a theatre coat. It was grey and hooded and lent her an odd fancy-dress appearance. She paused when she saw Frances and her black eyes wavered guiltily.

"The house is nice and warm," she remarked.

"Oh, darling, you shouldn't." The girl swept aside this flagrant attempt to divert the issue. "You ought not to come downstairs alone."

"My dear child." Old Mrs Ivory flushed with anger. "I may be old but I'm not yet in my grave, I
hope." She came forward confidently, remarkably
sure of herself, her small body held up by sheer
nervous strength. The ascent daunted her a little,
however, and she accepted her granddaughter's arm.
Frances found that she was trembling.

"Granny, you'll kill yourself," she said helplessly.
"What did you want down there? Couldn't I have
fetched it?"

Mrs Ivory paused on the stairs. She was breathless
and shaky, but her eyes were honestly furious.

"No, you could not," she said. "You're a nice girl.
You have my youth and my strength and my intelligence but you can't see for me. No one can see
for me with my eyes. No one can think for me. Oh,
my God, Frances, if I could steal your body how I
would!"

There was nothing whimsical about the final observation. Gabrielle was evidently speaking the literal
truth.

"Madam!"

Dorothea stood on the top of the stairs, her eyes
popping out of her head.

"Madam!" she said again, a world of fright and
reproach in her voice. "Oh, madam!"

She came down a step or two and Gabrielle relin-
quished Frances' arm and clutched the other woman.

"All right," she said and laughed. "All right,
Dorothea. No talk. No recriminations. Take me to
my room."

Dorothea did so quite literally. She bent her broad back, lowered her head and picked up her mistress, who appeared to be quite prepared for the treatment. Gabrielle was tiny. She rode like a child, one arm round the other woman's neck, and her own head nodding slightly in its little quilted hood.

"You go to the doctor, miss, while I get Madam settled." Dorothea spoke over her shoulder. "There's no one with him. Poor man, he must think it's a madhouse."

"Poor man," mimicked Gabrielle and gave one of her chuckles, which were still feminine and still spiteful.

Dorothea bore her away and Frances hurried down the hall to Phillida's room. She found the doctor outside the door, talking to Godolphin. They ceased abruptly as she came up and Godolphin nodded vigorously.

"I quite understand," he said. "I'll go across now and find somebody. Oh, my dear fellow, don't apologise. I agree with you. It's necessary, or at least it's wise. All right then, leave it to me."

He limped off, glad to be of some service.

"Did you get a nurse?" Frances put the question anxiously.

"Yes, I did." He smiled at her. "Two good women are coming along at once. I rather thought I'd go and fetch them myself, as a matter of fact."

"That's extremely nice of you."

"Not at all." He looked a little uncomfortable. "I shall have to have a word with them in private and I

thought I'd get it over in the car. Oh, and by the way,
I . . . er . . . I thought that just to placate everybody
and to put myself absolutely in the right with the
Nursing Agency that I might get one of these plain-
clothes men who are swarming about the place to go
on duty outside this door. Then the nurses can't feel
that they're in any dan . . . well, that there's anything
to be excited about, can they?"

He was watching her anxiously, and it came to her
how extraordinarily good he was being.

"It's only a super-precaution," he insisted. "Just a
courtesy to the agency."

"You mean no one could attack them from outside?" she murmured.

"I mean then no one could attack them at all, my
dear," he said briskly. "Mr Godolphin offered to fix
it. He's been very helpful. He's *the* Godolphin, isn't
he? What's his position here?"

A wild inclination to say, "He's Phillida's real
husband" and see what happened assailed Frances,
but she controlled it and answered cautiously.

"He's not a relative but he's a very old friend.
When he came back and found us in this mess and
heard that Daddy was held up in quarantine he
offered to stay and do what he could."

"Oh, I see." The doctor was satisfied. "Good of
him," he commented, but she fancied his glance was
thoughtful as he looked over his shoulder into the
bedroom, and she wondered what Phillida might have
let slip in that strange blurred muttering of hers.

With the departure of the doctor and the return of

Mrs Sanderson to keep vigil in the sickroom a temporary peace descended on the house. The plainclothes man was back at his post in the hall, and Godolphin had not yet returned from his mission to Bridie over at the gallery.

Frances went into her own room and sat down on the bed. For the first time she realised how weary she was. She was so tired that it was a relief to sit and listen to it. The old phrase brought her own mother back into her mind. Once in this house Meyrick's second wife used to sit and listen to the intolerable pain of her last illness. "You can get above it if you do," she had said to the bewildered child climbing onto her bed. "Listen to it and it's not yours. It's a thing by itself. When you're in pain, my darling, listen to it."

Frances listened to her weariness and to the dull tightness round her heart which was as real and physical a manifestation as if the organ was actually injured.

She was still sitting there when Dorothea found her. The old woman came in with a mumble of mingled relief and reproach and plumped herself down in the bedside chair.

"I'm sorry, miss," she said with that slight truculence which is born of fear, "I can't help it. I think my legs will give way any minute."

"Oh, Dorothea!" Frances scrambled off the bed, alarmed and contrite. "Dorothea, I'm so sorry. What can I get you? I forget that you're not younger than any of us. We all do."

"It's not the work; that's nothing. You sit down yourself, miss." Dorothea was breathing deeply and her square wrinkled face was pallid. "I'm as strong as ever I was, as I tell my niece when she comes nosing round to know why I don't leave service. No, it's not that. It's me heart."

She laid her hand on her stiff black bosom expressively.

"It's me heart," she repeated and shot a sidelong glance at the girl. "I love the mistress," she began after a pause. "If she was my own mother I couldn't love her more. I've been with her since I was a girl, since I was fifteen. I know her. I've seen her grow old."

She was silent and Frances, looking at her, was startled to see tears slip out of her eyes and slide down over her cheeks. Tears and wrinkles are ever an appalling combination, but in Dorothea, that tower of strength and common sense, they were terrifying. A drop fell on her hand, and she looked down at it in surprise.

"I'm off me head," she said, brushing her eyes angrily. "But, oh, Miss Frances, my dear, I'm so frightened. You see, it's not the first time I've found her wandering about this house."

"What?"

"There, there, my dear, don't get excited." Now that the admission was made and her secret out Dorothea was much more herself again. "It doesn't actually signify. But I must tell somebody for my own peace of mind. It's no good me talking to the

police; they'd only come and worry her and she's too
old for that. Besides, I won't have it. They bully her
over my dead body."

"But, Dorothea, what is this? What do you mean?
When did you find her wandering about the house
before? Not on the night . . ."

"Yes, I did. On the night Mr Robert must have
died. She was wandering about the house in the pitch
dark. She knows the place so well, you see. We lived
here for thirty years. You get to know a house in
that time."

Frances sat down abruptly. Her fine eyes were narrowed and there was a frightened stiffness in the set
of her mouth.

"You'd better tell me," she said.

Dorothea bent forward and lowered her voice to
the earnest monotone of confidence.

"Do you remember meeting me outside Miss
Phillida's door that night?" she said. "You remarked
that it was a pity the mistress had come and I said
yes, it was and that she was very angry with Mr
Robert. I know I told you then that she wouldn't go
to bed but was sitting by the fire talking about the
old days."

"I remember. Go on."

"I'm telling you. I went back to her then and she
seemed quieter, but still I couldn't get her to go to
bed anyhow. She wouldn't take this and she wouldn't
take that. I couldn't do a mortal thing with her. After
a bit I went out and left her. That always annoys her,
and I thought it might bring her to her senses. I

went down to the kitchen to get her a drop of hot milk. Norris was out that night, and I got talking with Mrs Sanderson and Molly. I don't know how long I was there, but it might have been well over an hour. Anyway, when I came back with the glass on a tray I found all the lights in the place were out."

"Who did that?"

"I don't know. At the time I thought Mr Robert had probably done it himself. I didn't really think at all except to be afraid that it was later than I thought. I didn't turn on the hall light myself because it wasn't as if I was at home, and I could get on just as well without it, considering the hundreds of times I've come up those stairs. I went across the landing and pushed open her door. 'Here I am,' I said and waited for her to say something pretty sharp to me."

She paused and looked at the girl with some of the bewilderment of that moment echoed in her eyes.

"She wasn't there. The room was empty. I couldn't believe it. She's been so helpless for the last year. I thought the effort of coming up here from Hampstead would be too much for her. Well, I was at my wit's end. I set the milk down and went out again. I didn't know what to do."

There was vividness in the old voice, and Frances saw her standing on the threshold of the big shadowy bedroom, the fire dying low behind her.

"I was afraid, you see." Dorothea's whisper was urgent. "I knew the house but I didn't know the people. Every room in the place was as well known

to me as the palm of my own hand, but I didn't know
who might be in any of them. There'd been one noise
in the house already, and I didn't want to make another."

"Noise?"

"Well, row, then. But it's not a nice word. Mr
Robert had forgotten himself to the mistress in the
afternoon. Poor fellow! When I heard he was dead
I was sorry but I could never have forgiven him for
the things he said to her that day if he'd lived to be a
hundred. There I was, wondering what on earth I
ought to do, when I heard her coming across the hall.
I knew it was her. I'd know her step anywhere. But
I couldn't believe my ears. I hadn't heard her walk
like that for twenty years. She was brisk, you know,
walking like a proper little madam. I ran to the top
of the stairs and called her softly because I didn't
want to rouse the house. 'Is that you?' I said. 'Yes,'
she said and her voice was young too. I thought I was
out of my mind. She was so angry, you see, it had
given her strength. I went down and found her and
brought her up to the fire. She was quite calm, not
at all shaky as she was tonight, but just calm and
wilful and wonderfully clear in her mind. That was
when she told me to send the cable."

"She told you *then?*"

"Of course she did." Dorothea prodded her listener's knee. "That was how I got the address. I tell you
she was ten years younger that night, although she
had to pay for it afterwards, poor dear. She was just
like she used to be, sharp as a needle, with every fact

she wanted slap at her finger tips. She remembered
Mr Meyrick had given her the Hong Kong cable
address and that it was in her black book in her writ-
ing case. She made me write out the message there
and then. 'Come home immediately. Your presence
vital in new development. Gabrielle.' That's how it
ran. I promised her I'd send it off the first thing the
next day. That's why I sent Molly to the post office
with it in the morning. I didn't have time to phone
it or to run out myself with the mistress lying there
exhausted."

"So Molly sent it? That's how the inspector heard
about it? Is that why you dismissed her when Robert
was found?"

Dorothea sniffed.

"Yes, that was a silly thing to do," she said. "I
lost my head. When he was found I lost my head. I
couldn't forget that she'd been about that night. I
don't know what I thought so don't ask me. I only
felt that I couldn't have the poor dear questioned,
and the simplest thing to do seemed to be to get rid
of the girl before she remembered anything. I went
down and packed her off. In my young days there'd
have been no questions asked and no reasons given.
I'd forgotten how things have changed. There was
such a setout you'd have thought I was getting rid of
a member of Parliament, let alone a housemaid. I
called attention to the whole thing instead of hiding
it up. I had to come and tell the mistress and she
acted us both out of it, the wonderful little old dear."

The quiet voice ceased and there was silence in the

room for a minute or so before Frances could bring herself to ask the question which was nagging at her.

"Dorothea," she began cautiously at last, "you didn't leave Gabrielle today, did you?"

"While she was in the picture gallery?"

"Yes."

The old woman leant back in her chair. Her face was drawn and her lips fidgeted for a while before she spoke.

"Only for a quarter of an hour," she said. "She was sitting in a chair and she dropped off to sleep, or I thought she did. You can't tell with her these days; she's so artful. I knew she wouldn't be disturbed there and I wanted to make sure they hadn't forgotten the fire in her bedroom. She'd been upset and I couldn't have her coming back to a cold room. I went back the way we came, past Mr Meyrick's door and down the back stairs. I got out into the yard and popped into our kitchen here. I talked for rather a long time with Norris and the other two. He said he'd just been up to see to the fire and it went through my mind that he might have been listening through that door in the cupboard.

"I don't know how much you can hear through that. Anyway, they pretended to be all agog to hear what had happened at the meeting and I was careful not to tell them. I suppose I was talking for over ten minutes, maybe quarter of an hour, maybe more. When I came back they'd found Mr Lucar and all the excitement was on."

"Was Granny awake when you got to her?"

"Yes. She was walking about the room. She was as bright as she is tonight. I noticed the change in her. It's almost as if these upsets give her a new interest in life."

Her voice died away and she sat thinking. After a while she laughed.

"I'm daft," she said. "She couldn't. It's silly. Even if her poor sweet mind had gone and she'd taken it into her head to do something so wicked, she couldn't. She hasn't the strength. It's us, Miss Frances. We're the lunatics. We're so muddled and frightened we're losing our sense. She couldn't do it. Besides, what with?"

Frances did not speak at once. A quotation from the flowery history book of her nursery days had come sneaking into her mind. "If but the blades be sharp enough a child can drive it home, my Lord Burleigh."

"Would she do it?" she demanded bluntly. "I mean, just supposing she could. Would she? Can you conceive her doing it?"

It was a rhetorical question, and she was prepared for a vigorous negative. Dorothea's reply was startling.

"Not unless she thought she was so old it didn't matter," she said.

"Didn't matter?" said Frances, aghast.

"What happened to her afterwards. Very old people are funny, miss. They've got so used to the idea of dying that they get to behaving sort of wild, like people going to emigrate. She's so clear in her

mind that this life is over for her that she's half living
in the next. I never knew anyone who treated their
body so much as if it was an old dress they were
wearing out. She's still young in her heart, you see,
still adventuresome. She's impatient, that's what she
is. I don't know what she might do."

"But she couldn't . . ."

"No, my dear, she couldn't, thank God." Dorothea
dried her eyes with a single wipe from the flat of her
hand. "I feel a mount better," she remarked naïvely.
"It's keeping it all to oneself that makes one fanciful.
Once it's in words you do know it's silly."

"Yet someone did it," Frances said slowly.

"Eh? Yes, yes, someone did it." Dorothea sounded
almost casual. "Still, *she's* safe from trouble, that's
all I care. She's sitting up by the fire. She's wonderfully wilful and very bright again tonight. I'll just go
along to see how Miss Phillida is. If we're going to
have nurses in the house that Mrs Sanderson must
help me tidy up the room a bit. You go along to your
granny, my dear. Tell her I'm just coming."

Her resilience was amazing. Confession seemed not
only to have been good for her soul but for her legs
also, for she rose to her feet briskly.

"Well, we must get on," she said. "I'll put the
nurses in the old playroom. It's warm up there by
the water tank. Don't you worry, my dear, it 'll all
come right."

Frances followed her to the door. They parted on
the landing and the girl turned towards Gabrielle's
room. She walked heavily. Dorothea might be able

to trot off happily to attend to mere domestic problems, but for her own part she found the new details
terrifying. Why had Gabrielle been wandering about
the house on the night that Robert died? Why? And,
above all, where?

She entered the dark alcove where Meyrick's door
was and had already raised her hand to tap on the
panelling when she heard Gabrielle talking. The high
thin voice was raised authoritatively and the words
came clearly through the wood and leather.

"All my life I have done what I thought best. I
see no reason to change that behaviour. Have you
ever been told that you look like the prince con-
sort?"

Frances felt her scalp crawling. As far as she knew
there was no one in the house who could possibly
be with the old lady.

She opened the door abruptly and went in. Gabrielle confronted her. She was seated facing the door in
a high-backed chair which had been temporarily
lined with her enormous swansdown shawl. The
lights were shaded and the glow from the coal fire
picked out the brilliance of her black eyes and the
rings on her fingers, while behind her the shadowy
forms of the bed and the armoire melted into the
warm darkness.

At first glance Frances thought that she was alone
and talking to herself and she was just facing the new
problem which such a discovery might well present
when the wing chair standing on the rug between
them shot back a little as a man rose up out of it.

"David!"

His sudden appearance was so unexpected that she forgot herself entirely and her voice rose. They both hushed her vigorously.

"I'm sorry," she whispered, reddening at the injustice which such treatment always seems to contain, "but I thought you were . . ."

"Arrested." Gabrielle supplied the missing word. "But he seems either to have been let out or to have escaped." She let her voice rise enquiringly but he did not explain. He stood on the hearthrug, his hands in his pockets and his head bent. Although the pose was negligent his shoulder muscles were flexed under his coat and there was an unusual tautness in the fine lines of his face.

Frances glanced at him anxiously and found him watching her thoughtfully, without smiling.

"I've been asking Mrs Ivory to shut the house," he said. "Split up. Pack the servants off. If Phillida's ill let her go into a nursing home. You can go to a hotel, Frances. Mrs Ivory herself can return to Hampstead. Get the house empty."

"What? Tonight?"

"Oh, lord yes, it must be tonight."

"But, David, we can't." In her reaction against the impracticability of the suggestion Frances forgot for a moment how extraordinary it was that he should be there at all. "We can't," she repeated. "Anyway, we're not allowed to. We're all to stay here until Inspector Bridie has finished with the gallery and can come over and interview us all again. There's a

policeman in the front hall and another on the back
door now. Didn't you see them as you came in?''

"No. I—er—I didn't come that way."

"I heard his tapping at the cupboard," explained
Gabrielle calmly. "I thought it was the police so I
let him in. He has not cared to explain how he came
to be in my son's private office." There was no rebuke
in her tone. She made the statement as if it referred
to some minor unconventionality into which she was
too polite to enquire.

Frances glanced at the small cupboard beside the
fireplace. The door was bolted again now. She could
see the brass catch clearly against the panelling.
David followed her eyes gloomily but he made no
comment, and it was the old lady who returned to the
main subject.

"Quite impossible," she said, resettling herself.
"And if it weren't I should still stay. There is something I want to know." Her voice had a new tone
in it and he turned to her. For a moment he looked
positively frightened, but as his eye took in her frailty
and her great age his alarm died a little.

"I hope you're not thinking of turning detective,
Mrs Ivory," he murmured.

The old Gabrielle appeared to consider the suggestion.

"No," she said at last. "No. But I'm a very inquisitive old woman, and in all this dreadful business
there is one thing that strikes me as very strange
indeed. First, Madrigal, poor wretched creature, is
found dead with a wound in his chest. Then that

abominable little baggageman dies in the same way. As far as any reasonable person can see both crimes were committed by the same person, who must be someone who is still either in this house or in the gallery next door. So much is obvious. Any woman who blinds herself to those facts is a fool. However, the thing that seems so entirely extraordinary to me is this: both houses have been searched over and over again and yet no weapon has been found. I find this so peculiar that I have given my mind to it, and an idea has occurred to me which may eventually explain a number of things."

The precise Victorian English and the conversational tone made the words unexpectedly dramatic.

"I am not going to tell you or anyone else what it is," she said, "because if I am wrong then I have made a very serious and unjust mistake. So I shall stay here until I find out for myself. What is the matter, Mr Field?"

David's eyes were warning and when he spoke his voice sounded dry.

"That's a very dangerous statement. Have you made it to anybody else?"

The old lady peered at him and then turned sharply to glance at the cupboard door beside her.

"Have you?" he repeated, raising his voice a little.

"No," she said. "No, I have not. But you come to me with a suggestion and I am explaining to you why I am not adopting it. Now, forgive me. I am tired. Frances will take you downstairs."

It was her usual dismissal, imperious and unanswerable. He moved obediently but when he was halfway across the room he turned again.

"You mustn't," he said. "For God's sake. Think of everybody else."

The black eyes flickered in his direction, and for an instant both young people saw her as she must have been at the height of her powers, when her brain was as clear as any in London and her tremendous vitality was a force in a great many lives.

"One more day," she said so quietly that her voice would not carry through any panelling. "One more day."

"What does she mean?" Frances whispered the question as they came out into the alcove. His hand closed over her arm warningly. He did not move but stood listening, holding her back in the shadow. No one was in sight, but all around them the house was alive. There were new voices downstairs and footsteps. She heard Godolphin talking and a strange woman answering him, and then the doctor spoke. David bent over her.

"Is there a fire escape to this house? Keep your voice down."

Frances stiffened. Until that moment she had not taken Gabrielle's airy statement about his escape from arrest with any degree of seriousness. He saw her expression and his eyes wavered.

"Sorry, Duchess," he murmured, "but it can't be helped. Where's the bolt hole?"

"Up here." She took his wrist and drew him hastily across the narrow end of the landing to the flight of steep stairs leading up to the third floor. Neither of them spoke until they were out on the roof, standing in a narrow valley beneath the shadow of a chimney stack. It was very dark up there. All the light came from below, giving new values and strange topsy-turvy shadows, while the fidgety wind leapt on them avidly, snatching at their clothes and blowing soot in their eyes.

Frances steadied herself in the guttering.

"You go straight along here," she said huskily, ridiculously concerned because her teeth were chattering. "Then over the parapet to the next house—it's only offices so there's no one there now to hear you—then the iron ladder goes down at the back of the house. You'll have to drop the last eight feet, but it 'll be all right if you're careful."

"I see. Thank you." He did not move and she could not see his face.

"Well?" she said at last.

His hand found her shoulder and closed over it. He did not speak for a long time but he rocked her gently, his fingers gripping her very tight.

"Come with me."

"Where?"

"Holland. God knows what I'm letting you in for, but come and we'll risk it. . . . It's pure selfishness on my part."

"Why?"

He laughed explosively.

"Oh, darling," he said, "at such a time! Are you coming?"

"How can I? Phillida's ill, Gabrielle's alone—I can't. I must stay with them."

He let her go.

"Yes," he said unexpectedly. "Yes, of course." And then, with more urgency than she had ever heard from him before, "Frances. Be careful. Don't hear anything. Don't think anything. And for God's sake don't say anything. Watch Gabrielle. Never let her be left alone, not for a minute. Do you understand?"

"Yes. What are you afraid of?"

"I'm not." He spoke passionately. "That's the line you've got to drop. Drop it. Rout it out. Forget it. Turn yourself into a mindless vegetable. Don't think. Don't put two and two together. And keep Gabrielle quiet. Put her to bed and lock the door with yourself on the inside."

"You're going to Holland?"

He swore softly in the darkness.

"I shouldn't have told you that. That's the slip we all make. That's unforgivable. That's the one thing you must never tell anyone. Never, whatever happens. Promise. Word of honour."

"Yes," she said flatly. "Yes, of course. Word of honour."

She heard him move irresolutely, and then unexpectedly he bent over and kissed her, holding her so roughly that in spite of her fierce and rather terrifying relief she was aware that he was hurting her. The next moment he had left her and was clambering purposefully over the roofs.

17

"THEY BROADCAST AN UNFORTUNATELY
good description of him over the air in the ten-to-
twelve news last night. Silly chap. He can't hope to
get away with it. The country's too small," said
Godolphin gloomily and pushed his plate away.

The breakfast room at 38 Sallet Square was stuffy
and the electric light made the hour, which was noon,
seem unlikely and in keeping with the timeless con-
fusion of the whole period. Frances, who was sitting
on the other side of the table, her chin in her hands
and an untasted cup beside her, thought of the previous midnight as an age away, an undefined moment
in a horrible and distant past. It had been twelve
hours of mounting strain. The house was in chaos.
The domestic routine had broken down utterly, and a
sense of siege was everywhere.

On the news of the second crime the crowds in the
street had returned in greater numbers, and the heavy
old-fashioned shutters barred over the breakfast-
room windows made a temporary barrier between the
stricken household and the sensation seekers standing
patiently in the rain and the wind of the square.

The meal was a formless hybrid, midway between

breakfast and luncheon. Mrs Sanderson had done what she could at a time when food seemed one of the least important of life's considerations, and Norris, a bilious wraith of his former urbanity, had tottered up from the kitchen bearing a tray on which odd china and tarnished silver presented a collection of cold sausages, potatoes in their jackets, ham, jam and coffee.

The hall and landings had become foreign territory. The police possessed them, newspapermen stormed them, and every now and again a strange nurse in starched linen and sensible shoes crackled through them on her way to the kitchen.

Inspector Bridie had made a thorough search of both houses, and in his vocabulary the adjective had a particular meaning. His search had included the space beneath the floor boards, the contents of the mattresses, and the drains. So far it had been fruitless. The weapon which had killed Robert Madrigal and afterwards Henry Lucar had disappeared as completely and unsatisfactorily as if it had never existed.

No one in the house had had anything faintly approaching a night's rest. The interminable questionings had gone on hour after hour and mere nerves had given place to a state of grim endurance. Even Godolphin had begun to show the scars of the ordeal. There was a white line of excitement round his mouth, and when he limped about the hand which gripped his stick was heavily veined under the yellow skin.

Frances had no idea what she looked like and did

not care. Old Bridie, who was beginning to fear that
he almost liked her, had seen a white ghost of a
creature with great pain-filled eyes and had sent it in
to get something to eat with every ounce of his
authority behind the command.

"Silly young ass," Godolphin repeated under his
breath and sat up when he saw the spasm of pain
flicker over her face. "Sorry," he said abruptly.
"Wouldn't have mentioned it if I'd known. I understood that engagement of yours was a put-up job.
I shouldn't have said it for worlds if I'd thought."

He was looking at her with great interest in his
dark eyes, and she noticed, as one does notice irrele-
vant details in time of stress, that the whites of them
were still yellow from his fever.

His discovery seemed to awaken his energy again
for he bent towards her earnestly.

"You're kidding yourself, you know," he said.
"You're young so you don't realise it. Love does get
one but there's nothing in it. You'd get bored to
tears with that chap Field if you knew him for long.
He's a painter. All painters have a sort of romantic
glow round them, but they're silly, oversensitive
beggars when you get to know them. Impractical, too.
Look at this wild flight of his. What's he got to fear?
There's not a shred of evidence against him that the
police could prove. You're well rid of him. I don't
expect you to agree with me now but you will.
You'll see. You're a sensible girl. Besides, I mean to
say, take love altogether. I know it. It's a tremendous
thing while it lasts but it goes. That's the thing to

remember about love. You love like hell for years and then you see the woman again and you see her in a new light."

Frances took a long deep breath. The full force of the famous personality was like a blast from an oven. She felt dizzy and physically sick.

He hoisted himself onto another chair nearer to her and, seeing him prepare for a new attack, she drew back involuntarily. He was not being intentionally unkind but an idea had occurred to him and, as usual, he was bent on putting it over.

"If only he had had the sense to sit tight," he said. "Suppose it had come to a trial. Wouldn't you have backed him? Wouldn't I? Wouldn't Phillida and even the old lady? Of course we would, if only to save our own faces. A balanced chap would have seen that."

It occurred to Frances that she was going to cry. The discovery appalled her and she rose to her feet, choking. As she turned blindly to the door, however, it opened and Miss Dorset appeared with Dorothea in tow. Both women were exhausted and untidy in that odd way which is not definable. Miss Dorset in particular conveyed a dishevelment which was as much mental as any matter of coiffure or shoestrings.

"I made her come down," she said breathlessly. "She must eat something or she'll drop. You've got some coffee here, Norris says."

"Of course we have." Frances set a chair for the old woman as she spoke. Dorothea was exhausted, but a lifetime's training seemed to forbid her to sit on more than two inches of the proffered seat, since she was in company.

"I didn't ought to be down here," she grumbled, taking a cup grudgingly, "but she is dozing now, though, and that Mrs Sanderson has promised to stay with her. What a night it's been. I don't think she's closed her eyes once and it was all I could do to keep her in the room. It 'll kill her in the end, this will. It stands to reason. I've told her she's more like an obstreperous child than an old lady. She's got something on her mind, you know. She's overexcited. I thought she was going to fly out of the bed when the police asked if Miss Dorset could come through the cupboard door."

Both Frances and Godolphin looked up at this piece of information and Miss Dorset flushed.

"The inspector thought it would be better if I avoided the street," she murmured. "The crowd is waiting, hoping to see a woman."

Frances sat up. "Me?" she demanded.

Miss Dorset leant forward and laid a hand over hers.

"It's Mr Field running away," she said gently. "They don't *think*, you know. They just get hold of a dramatic idea. Never mind. It's all going to be all right. It's all going to be all right. I've just heard and I had to come over. Mr Meyrick's been released and he's coming back. He left this morning and we shall have him here any time after four. I nearly broke down and cried when I saw the message. It's what I've been praying for."

She looked positively happy and the others exchanged glances. Dorothea put the general thought into words.

"I'll be most relieved to see him, but I don't know what he can do, poor man," she remarked, sipping her coffee. "It's past anyone doing much, if you ask me."

"But there 'll be someone to tell us what to do." Miss Dorset sounded as if she had nothing more to ask. Her confidence was so sublime that they were encouraged in spite of themselves, and the atmosphere grew momentarily less oppressive. Nevertheless they all started violently when someone tapped on the door.

It was Bridie himself. He too had been up all night and had not had time to shave, but, apart from a slight greyness round his chin, he looked as neat and affably suspicious as ever. He disconcerted everyone by saying nothing at all, but he accepted Frances' offer of coffee with a nod of such alacrity that she began to suspect that it was his sole reason for intruding upon them. His presence silenced the three women, but Godolphin seized the opportunity to ask questions.

"Any news of Field yet?" he enquired, fixing the older man with inquisitive eyes.

"Not a wor-rd of him, silly young chuggins." The inspector seemed to be in an ominously genial mood, and his soft Northern voice was alarming in its friendliness.

"Do you think you'll get him?"

"Oh yes, no doubt about that. It's chust a question

of time. It's a tickens of a chob to escape us." Bridie
dismissed the question as ridiculous. "It's these
wretched chournalists who're the bother," he added,
peering round at them with his bright hooded eyes.
"Most tenacious chaps. There was one on the roof
chust now, and no young lady to help him either."

He laughed at Frances as he made the remark but
ignored the colour which came into her face. Nor did
he seem in the least annoyed with her. His manner
altered abruptly, however, as he turned to Dorothea.

"Where's your mistress?" he demanded.

"Mrs Sanderson is with her, sir."

"She is? Oh well, she's a sensible body. All the
same——"

He broke off as the door opened and Inspector
Withers put his head in. His long face was lined with
anxiety.

"There's a young man out here says he must see
Mr Godolphin on a matter of life or death," he said
suspiciously.

"Really?" The explorer took his stick and hoisted
himself to his feet. "Who is it? What does he say?"

"He won't speak." Withers sounded irritable.
"He's simply waiting here, swearing that it's urgent.
He's got past two of our men."

"I'll come. Where is he? In the hall?"

Godolphin hobbled out at a great speed, and the
two officials exchanged glances, after which Withers
nodded and followed him. Evidently the residents
of 38 Sallet Square were not to have private inter-
views with any visitor that morning.

Bridie passed his empty cup to his hostess with engaging diffidence.

"I'm not a great drinker as a cheneral rule," he remarked, "but a chob like this makes one thirsty." His new friendliness was disconcerting, and Frances' hand shook as she held the saucer. The rattling cup attracted his attention and he smiled at her kindly. "Cheer up," he said. "It's a fe-ear-rful business but we're near-ring the finish. There's absolutely no question about that. There's chust a little anxiety for the next few hours, but you'll all be able to sleep easy in your beds tonight without a chance of being murdered there."

"Can you say that definitely, Inspector?" Miss Dorset was leaning across the table, her ugly light eyes eager.

Bridie looked at her squarely. "Quite definitely," he said. "Four o'clock, that's the hour. We'll all know a great deal more about this chiggery-pokery at four o'clock, and by the way, Miss Dorset, for your own infor-rmation, all the telephone lines in this house and the next are tapped and have been for some time."

The effect on the woman of this gratuitous piece of information was astonishing, and Bridie watched her with pleasure as his little trap sprang home. She grew very white, all except for her nose and the red rims round her eyes. She closed her lips tightly and shrank back into her chair.

The moment was saved most unexpectedly by a great bellow of laughter outside the door as Withers

and Godolphin came in together. Both men were
amused, Godolphin rather sourly so but the inspector
guffawing openly. Bridie regarded him with sober
disapproval.

"Having a cholly good choke?" he enquired acidly.

"Yes sir." Withers recovered his habitual gloom.
"It was the chap's optimism," he added and Godolphin laughed briefly.

· "The fool of a motor salesman from the showrooms
down the road," he said. "I've been considering a
new Packard and they gave me a trial run in it yesterday, as I told you. It was when I came back that I
found the house in uproar. Apparently I had promised
to phone this youngster in the morning but naturally
I hadn't given the matter another thought."

"He got past the men on the door," murmured
Withers. "Some salesman."

Godolphin grunted. "He won't come back for a
bit now," he said grimly. "That sort of thing always
irritates me. Any man with a grain of intelligence
would have realised that this wasn't the time to
badger a prospective customer."

"It must mean a very big commission to him,"
muttered Miss Dorset.

"Of course it is, considerable." Godolphin was
contemptuous. "That's why it's so silly to jeopardise
it."

They were all in that state of near exhaustion when
trivial disagreements could easily have flared into
downright quarrels and Bridie put down his cup with
a rattle.

"Ah well," he said, rising, "the young lad was an hour or so too early, that's all."

"Four o'clock," said Frances with a sigh.

"Four o'clock," repeated the Scotsman, watching Miss Dorset.

Inspector Withers looked scandalised and Frances added a new piece of information to her store. Bridie was giving away an official secret. She wondered why.

"Oh, that's zero hour, is it? I hadn't heard that," put in Godolphin. "What are we to expect meantime?"

"Nothing, please God." Bridie spoke fervently but was not rewarded for his piety, for the door burst open almost immediately, admitting a very angry woman.

Nurse King was a thickset woman with a dark-skinned face and heavy brows meeting across her forehead. Her uniform might have been made of stiff white paper from the noise it made, and the hands which appeared beneath her glistening cuffs were scarlet and very strong. She was not a person who was used to defeat, and her present state of indignation and alarm had also a modicum of astonishment in it. She stood in the doorway, looking about her a trifle wildly.

"I must resign," she said. "If I'm to have no authority, if I'm to be ordered here and there like a servant, if I'm to be called this and that and turned out of my own patient's room as if I were a paid spy, I must go. That's all there is for me to do. No one would stand for it and no one can expect me to."

"Of course not." Frances was already halfway across the room towards the woman. "Of course not, nurse. She's ill, though. It's the frightful shock. Didn't the doctor tell you? She doesn't know what she's saying, I'm sure of that."

"Even so"—Nurse King was threatening to become hysterical, a condition so foreign to her nature that she did not recognise it—"even so, Miss Ivory, I'm entitled to a little consideration. I've had a difficult time with Mrs Madrigal without being ordered about by a second patient."

"Chimminy!" Bridie upset a chair as he lunged forward. "Who are ye talking about, woman?"

"Oh, I'm not complaining about my patient." The nurse flushed a dusky scarlet at the suggestion. "I'm not likely to mind anything my patient says, I hope. But when one of the household comes in and orders me out as if I were a probationer I do have something to say. 'No listening at the door, my good woman,' she says. 'Be off with you. No impudence.' I've never been spoken to like it in my life."

"Gabrielle!" Frances ejaculated. "Mrs Sanderson must have left her."

"Ma God!" The words broke from Bridie as he turned and fled out into the hall with Withers behind him.

His reaction was revealing and they all followed, swarming up the broad staircase, yet a new fear clutching at their skirts. They passed Withers on the landing. He was in a corner talking bitterly in a low voice to the plain-clothes man who had been on duty outside the sickroom. The detective was grovelling, clearly incapable of explaining how it was that an old woman should have been able to intimidate him.

The bedroom door was open and, with Dorothea leading, they filed in. Phillida was lying back among the pillows, her face as white as the linen, while on the end of the bed, calm, obstinate and completely mistress of the situation, sat a Gabrielle whom no one had ever seen before. She had shrunk, settling down inside herself until she looked like a netsuke, swathed in white lace wool. Her frailty was no longer her dominant feature. Instead she had become minute and vital, a concentrated essence of herself. Her face was so wrinkled that it was ageless and unreal, like the faces of ancient Italian peasant women, and her black eyes were bright and dangerous.

Bridie stood looking at her with something that was almost like superstition, and they realised for the first time how much the incident had shaken him. Frances looked anxiously at Phillida, but the dull-eyed woman in the bed made no sign of recognition and she called the nurse, who bustled over to the bed and put her foot down after a single glance. The room must be cleared instantly, she said, or she could not be responsible.

Her anxiety impressed even Bridie, who cleared his throat.

"We'll have to have an end of all this," he said, speaking slowly and quietly, his magnificent accent lending the words a softness which they do not ordinarily possess. "There's no question about it.

For a few hours I've got to have ye all under ma eyes and since I can't be in two places at once I'll have ye all together, everybody, servants and all. We'll all go down to the drawing room and we'll set there together until four o'clock."

"Not *her*." Dorothea forgot her place for the first time in a life in what she was pleased to call "gentleman's service." Her square face was suffused with blood and her body shook with the violence of her protest. "She shan't. She goes down there over my corpse. She's old. She's not herself. Her mind's not right. Can't you see yourself she's too old to be tormented? She'll work herself up and say things she doesn't know she's saying. I'll take her back to her room. She's fanciful She's old. You can't judge her like anyone else. You take her over my dead body."

"Thank you, Dorothea, that will do." The thin voice was icily amused. "I shall certainly go down to the drawing room, as the inspector suggests. There are one or two things I should very much like to say."

Bridie was looking at her in undisguised astonishment.

"I don't think you were very well, ma'am, last time I had a chat with you," he ventured.

Gabrielle favoured him with one of her more exquisite smiles.

"Perhaps I was not," she said. "Age is a curious malady, my dear man. There are times when one almost recovers from it."

Bridie's eyes flickered, and the old lady laughed as if she had made a conquest.

A slight movement on the other side of the room caught the policeman's attention, and he turned round just in time to see Miss Dorset edging towards the door. She stopped dead in her tracks as he called her and turned to face him defiantly, like a child.

"You'll hardly need me," she said.

He did not speak at once but stood looking at her until her colour changed.

"Chust the same," he said, "I'd like ye to be there."

"But I can't. I have an appointment just after three-thirty."

"Ye've got an appointment now. If ye were thinking of meeting Mr Meyrick Ivory's train, I'm sorry but I'll have to ask ye to change yer mind."

She hesitated and for a moment it looked as if she were thinking of defying him. He watched her thoughtfully.

"There's an extension telephone in the drawing room," he said. "I'll arrange for all your business calls to be put through there."

The simple offer, with the slight emphasis on the word "business," had its effect. Miss Dorset stood blinking at him, a foolish expression on her face so unlike her usual birdlike glance that it was frightening.

"Very well," she said huskily and turned slowly out of the room, a crushed and submissive figure.

18

THEY TROOPED INTO THE DRAWING ROOM
like an old-fashioned household going in to family
prayers. There was the same hush, the same furtive
reluctance. Norris turned on the lights, for the winter
afternoon was dark, and the haste with which Mrs
Sanderson and Molly pulled the heavy window
curtains reminded everyone afresh of the patient
crowds outside. Frances felt a little sick whenever
she thought of them. The morbid aspect of their
behaviour as individuals had long since ceased to
impress her. She saw them now as the representatives
of the public, the rest of the herd, patiently waiting
for the law of the tribe to be enforced. Two men had
been killed and they had a right to expect that the
murderer should be apprehended, tried and finally
hanged. They were taking no part in the time-
honoured ritual but were standing by to see that it
was performed. Their presence threw the whole
affair into relief, so that even as she took part in it
she saw it also objectively, like a scene on a lighted
stage.

Gabrielle took the largest chair by the fire and
Dorothea stood beside her. Nothing would persuade
her to sit down, and she remained, solid and formi-

dable, between her mistress and the rest of the room.

Frances sat in a corner of a chesterfield, with Godolphin perched stiffly on the arm beside her, while Miss Dorset placed herself next to the occasional table where the telephone stood. The three servants sat together near the door. They had arranged themselves in order of seniority and succeeded in looking like a small jury in their effort to appear intelligent yet nothing to do with the case.

It was when Bridie had taken up his own position behind the Louis XV table, with Withers at his elbow, that Frances first became nervously aware of the clock. The gilt sunburst with the garden face was as familiar to her as the room itself, but today it was a new and menacing thing.

It was half-past two, later than she had thought, and she moved uneasily in her quilted corner. There was a tremendous sense of constriction in the room. No one breathed easily, and the entire gathering was aware of that tingling sensation in the soles of the feet which comes just before the worst is told.

Frances stared resolutely at the fire. It was like being in a plane which had lost its undercarriage, she decided. Enough juice for another hour and a half before the crash and meanwhile nothing to do but wait.

Bridie's sibilant voice cut into her thoughts.

"It's against all the rules of police procedure for me to question any witness in front of another," he was saying pleasantly. "There's absolutely no question about that. However, I'm not proposing to

keep ye here in silence until four o'clock so I've decided to give ye a sor-rt of cheneral lecture on the
two crimes, and when I come to any bit that I'm
not so sure about then I shall expect your intelligent
coöperation."

His simple words and confiding smile were so
naïve that they were almost deceived, all, that is,
save Frances, who had seen the old Scot in this
particular dangerous mood once before.

"Excellent," said Gabrielle distinctly, just enough
patronage in her tone to remind the inspector ef-
fectively of the great ladies of the North when he
had been a child. He glanced at her sharply but
comforted himself, as he had done then, with the
recollection of his infinite mental superiority.

"Noo," he said, glancing about him with the bland
affability which was so misleading, "since ye're none
of ye professionally skilled in the ar-rt of investi-
gation I'll commence ma observations with a few
cheneral remarks. In this particular affair, which is
all the more shockin' to ye since ye're all so close to
it, I want ye to get into your minds a lar-rge square
of boar-rd on which there is a half-finished chigsaw
puzzle. Ye can see by the shape of the hole which is
left that ye need a human heid to complete the
picture."

He paused and his bright eyes swept round the
gathering with horrific good humour.

"A human heid with a recognisable face."

It was an oddly unpleasant simile and, coming on
top of the strain which was already so great, its

effect was unnerving. Bridie seemed quite pleased
with it, however, for he continued happily.

"The missing pieces of the chigsaw are held by
different indiveeduals, and most of them are in this
room, no question about that. Each pairson con-
seedering his own piece of puzzle is confronted by a
wee mystery, but as soon as they're all on the table
together the little chuts and corners will begin to fit
and gradually the face will appear. It's cholly
inchenious."

"Cholly good work, sir," murmured Godolphin
under his breath to Frances, who did not hear him.
Her eyes were on the clock. Fifteen minutes gone
already.

"Hooever," Bridie swept on, "the fir-rst thing to
do is to define the outline of the heid. That's the
main conseederation. The background of the picture
has to be built up fir-rst, and the main ar-rt of this
piece of construction is to weed out all unnecessary
matter—mebbe I'm too complicated for ye?"

"On the contrary." Gabrielle's voice was sharp.
"We find you extraordinarily clear. Go on."

"I'm glad to hear it, ma'am," said Bridie with
what appeared to be innocent satisfaction. "We'll
now descend to the parteecular. Over three weeks
ago Mr Robert Madrigal disappeared. A week later
his body was discovered and on the same day Henry
Lucar sailed for New York. As soon as he received
wor-rd of the occurrence he returned, hooever, of
his own free will. He was examined by the police
and permitted to go home. The following day he

called a conference of the relations and associates
of Robert Madrigal and was himself mysteeriously
mur-rdered by the same weapon which had killed
his chief. This perneecious act took place only a few
minutes after that gathering had broken up and
while most of it was still in the gallery. That's an
undisputed fact. We noo cut out the unnecessary
factor-r. The murder of Henry Lucar does not merit
our immediate conseederation and I'll tell ye for why.
Henry Lucar was a blackmailin' scoundrel, no question of that. We have evidence to show that during
his lifetime Robert Madrigal paid out conseederable
sums of money which coincided in amount and date
with sums paid into Lucar's account. We also know
that chust before Mr Madrigal disappeared he and
Lucar were both present in the gallery when one of
Mr Field's pictures was slashed by an unknown
hand. This was the last of several such incidents and
the inference is that Lucar did the mischief to for-rce
Mr Madrigal to face up to the fact that he was
seerious in some last and more ineequitous demand.
It was a show of strength, d'ye see?"

"Yes." Frances bit the word off hastily and the
old man beamed at her.

"It's a bit of a chumble," he said, "but it soon
straightens oot. Well, Lucar was a blackmailer and
so it was never likely that he did away with Mr
Madrigal before he'd squeezed all the chuice out of
him. Moreover, I am convinced that Lucar left England before he knew for cer-rtain that Madrigal was
deid. As soon as the news reached him he scuttled

home, proved his alibi beyond question, and set off
to blackmail again. What hold he had over Mr
Madrigal we do not know, but we do know the
almighty secret he shared with someone else. He
knew who had killed Madrigal, ye see? As soon as
he heard the man was deid he knew who had killed
him, and when he called that conference this time
yesterday afternoon he made the fact cholly plain to
someone in that room. Whether he made it clear to
the murderer or to an accomplice of the murderer
does not matter. He let out that he knew the truth,
and within an hoor he was deid himself. That's a
simple story. We've got the motive and in time we'll
get the pairson concer-erned, but for the moment
we can disregai-rd Lucar altogether. When we get
the one heid filled in that picture will do for the
other chigsaw as well."

He paused and looked up at the clock and every
eye in the room followed him. It was five past three.
Miss Dorset blew her nose and the servants shuffled
uneasily. The emotional temperature in the room
was rising to fever heat.

"The main picture," continued Bridie calmly,
"concairns Robert Madrigal, as it always did. A
great many of the chigetty bits are in ma own hands
and already I've built up ma surround. The fir-rst
piece we need is a question of motive. The textbooks
tell us there are seventeen motives for mur-rder,
but I've never bothered ma heid about mor-re than
three—love, money and revenge. And the principal
one in ma expeerience is money. It 'll probably sur-

prise one or two of ye to hear that ye all had the pest
money motives in the wor-rld for killing Madrigal."

He made the final statement conversationally, as
if he were relating some interesting academic point,
and hurried on before anyone could protest.

"He was ruining ye all. Unless something drastic
was done he'd have steered the fir-rm into liquidation.
Some of ye know this and some of ye don't, but for
the purpose o' clarity I'm going to have it all oot on
the table. Some years ago Robert Madrigal put his
entire for-rtune into the fir-rm of Ivory, which had
suffered badly both in the war and in the slump. By
doing so he acquired very conseederable executive
powers and from the very fir-rst he proved a dangerous and unbusinesslike pairson. Isn't that so, Miss
Dorset?"

"Yes, from the beginning." The woman's voice
stuck in her throat and came out hoarsely, so that
they all looked at her.

"Mr Meyrick Ivory was deeply concairned, naturally," Bridie went on placidly. "In the airly days,
when repeated cautioning proved of no avail, he did
his best to—shall we say—divairt Mr Madrigal's
attention and even persuaded him to take par-rt in
an overseas chourney. When he retur-rned, however,
he undid much of the good wor-rk which had been
accomplished in his absence. His chief fault seems
to have been chittering obstinacy. In most cases
where a divairgence of opeenion occurs between
two par-rtners chenerally one o' them raised capital
to buy the other pairson out, and this Mr Ivory seems

to have attempted several times in the past two years. Hooever, Mr Madrigal was always obstinate. Even in the face of his losses he stuck to his conveection that it was Mr Ivory's consairvatism and not his own unorthodox goings on which was lettin' the fir-rm doon. His wife implor-red him to be reasonable, but he refused and there the matter stood when Mr Ivory went to China. He had lechitimate and important business there, don't forget that. A very fine collection o' paintings on silk, the property o' the impeerial government, were aboot to come into the mar-rket and he was anxious to be on the spot. Meanwhile Mr Madrigal remained in charge. Wi' his senior par-rtner away he became more and more deeficult. He drew large sums out of the business, which we now see went directly to Lucar, and his cheneral behaviour caused conseederable alar-rm wherever it was understood."

His soft voice ceased for a moment, and he took out his watch and laid it on the table before him, so that the lid of the hunter case screened its face from the nearest of them.

"Well," he said, "there are few things more demoralising than to see one's bread and butter deleeberately wasted by a fool over whom one has no control. Some fools can be managed. They can be inveigled or startled into common sense. But there is one type o' fool who is impossible. By hook or by crook he has got hold o' the tiller o' the boat and his temperament is such that he'll run her on the rocks rather than let anyone else take a hand at steer-ring.

That is the kind of fool who makes the meekes among
us tur-rn to thoughts o' violence. A great fir-rm has
as many traditions as a great school or a great regi-
ment, and it often inspires the same kind of chealous
loyalty. I only mention this because there were quite
a number of pairsons intimately concairned with the
fir-rm who knew the real state o' affairs. Miss Dorset
knew, of course. So did Mrs Madrigal. And so did
you, Mrs Ivory, unless I'm mistaken."

"Yes, I knew," said old Gabrielle quietly. "I knew."

If Bridie was pleased by the admission he did not
show it. Like the famous heathen Chinese, whom he
was beginning to resemble more and more at every
dragging moment, his smile was childlike and bland.

"It wouldn't surprise me to hear-r that ye confided
yer worries to your lifelong pairsonal attendant."

"I knew," said Dorothea stolidly and regarded
him with unwinking eyes.

"And *you*." Bridie swung round on Norris. "You've
been in sairvice here for twenty years. Mebbe the
situation was not unknown to you."

Norris staggered to his feet. He was green with
nervousness and his words slurred and bubbled over
each other.

"I have enjoyed Mr Meyrick's confidence for a
number of years, sir. I think I did know a little of—
of the matter."

"Ha!" Bridie's eyes glanced from his own watch
to the clock and back again. It was ten past three.
"Mr Meyrick, he knew. Mr Meyrick Ivory knew.
He was the principal pairson involved. He went off

to China; that is to say he left England four-rteen
weeks before Madrigal met his death. When I was a
young man China was as far away as the stars,
almost, and even noo a great many of us are inclined
to think of it as a remote continent only vaguely connected with the Wester-rn hemispheere. However,
with the coming of the new aeroplane distance has
ceased to exist, as ye might say. Let me read you a
few interesting facts. By Impeerial Airways Hong
Kong to Bangkok takes four-rteen hours only. From
Bangkok to Calcutta the flying time is nine and a
half. From Calcutta to Karachi is another nine hours,
and it is possible to fly from Karachi to Southampton
by ordinary passencher plane in less than three days.
This is not evidence. It's chust another little bit o'
the chigsaw which may not fit in with the rest and
I only . . . "

"I protest."

The formal yet melodramatic objection from the
other side of the room shook the already electric
atmosphere with explosion force and they all turned
to look at Miss Dorset, who had risen, her face
patched red and white and her lips dangerously
unsteady. In the moment of absolute silence which
followed the telephone on the table beside her began
to ring, its shrill voice screaming noisily in the breathless room. Bridie smiled.

"Take yer call," he said.

They watched her as she took up the receiver and
saw her hand tremble and the blank, frozen expression growing on her face as she listened.

"Yes," she said. "Yes, Miss Dorset here. Yes, I did enquire. Messrs Ivory Limited, Sallet Square. Yes. Yes. Yes. I see. Yes. Thank you."

She put down the receiver very slowly and the click of the disconnecting wires was heard clearly all over the room.

"Well?" Bridie enquired. "And did ye get your answer?"

She tried to speak but gave it up and nodded.

"And your suspeecions were correct?"

"I—I—— Oh, I don't know. Don't ask me." Miss Dorset collapsed in her chair and covered her face with her hands.

Bridie regarded her with soft-eyed sympathy which might or might not have been genuine.

"Poor body," he said, adding almost without punctuation, "we noo have to conseeder the night o' the crime. The last pairson known to have seen Robert Madrigal alive is David Field."

Although she had been waiting for it the name jolted Frances unbearably and again she looked at the sunburst clock and saw that the gilt hands had reached the bottom of the circle and were creeping up again. Bridie glanced at her thoughtfully and continued, his sibilant accent caressing each word as it left his mouth.

"Ye all know what happened. Mr Field came to talk to Mr Madrigal about his engagement to Miss Frances Ivory and both men went into the garden room together where the blinds were not doon. What some of ye may not know is that Henry Lucar joined

them there and he and Mr Field had a few wor-rds.
Not unnaturally Mr Field objected to Henry Lucar's
inclusion at such a delicate conference. Lucar had a
wretched manner which charred on Mr Field's
susceptibeelities and he disposed of him pretty
sharply. Lucar went. Field is a for-rmidable pairson
for all his arteestic profession, and the wee ratty
Lucar soon took to his heels. What happened next is
parteecularly interesting. Madrigal, frightened at
the way Lucar had been treated, apprehensive because of the hold the man had over him, ye see, lost
his heid entirely and said something to Field. I have
the exact wor-rds here. According to the evidence
which I have collected Madrigal tur-rned to Field
and said: 'Ye've waited a long time for a woman wi'
money and now ye're not taking any chances, are
ye?'"

He paused and glanced round the room.

"Not a very nice obsairvation."

"My God, how like him," murmured Godolphin.
"David hit him, I suppose?"

"He did." Bridie nodded his approval at the right
answer. "He hit him on the chaw, scraping his own
knuckles and putting the man clean out for an
instant so that he fell on the floor. At least that's
Field's story. But Miss Ivory herself, who happened
to be in the yar-rd about that time or a few seconds
after, said she saw the two of them standing talking.
Would ye like to retract that statement, Miss Ivory?
It's very clear why ye made it."

"Yes, I would." Frances made the admission

huskily and Bridie nodded at Withers, who began
to write.

The Scot went on.

"This method of sifting the pieces is unor-rthodox
but it's remarkably effeecient. We're getting on verra
nicely with our afternoon's divairsion," he observed
with horrific geniality. "The shape o' the heid is
taking place before our eyes. The pieces are chump-
ing into poseetion. To retur-rn to the two men in the
garden room: there was Madrigal lying in the chair
where Field had lifted him, a disfiguring contusion
swelling up on his face. There was Field standing
before him, looking down."

The phrase touched Frances through the numb
wretchedness which was slowly consuming her. If
David had not made a dash for it. If only he had done
what even Godolphin saw was the intelligent thing
and had stayed to face the enquiry. She looked at the
clock again. Twelve minutes. Only twelve minutes.

Bridie was proceeding with his unhurried narrative.

"Accor-rding to his story Field went out into the
hall and fetched Madrigal's hat and coat. He also
tur-rned out the hall lights because they intended
to go out the other way. Madrigal was naturally
anxious not to be seen in his condeetion and Field
was not keen on the story being broadcast either, for
he was an impulsive chap wi' a reputation for hittin'
oot. The arrangement was that they should go down
to a doctor together to get the face patched up a bit.
Field left the hat and coat in the room, pulled down
the blinds, and then went upstairs to say good night

to his young lady, a fact which she corroborates.
He was with her a matter of five minutes and then
he came doon to the room again."

He paused and looked at them all consideringly.

"From this point," he said, "his story becomes
very impor-rtant, because if it's not true then there's
only one conclusion we can draw from his lying. He
says his hand was already on the gar-rden-room door
when he hear-rd Madrigal speaking to someone
inside. The wor-rds were quite distinct and he remembered them. According to Field, Madrigal said,
'Why on airth did ye come here at this moment of
all times?' I'll repeat the phrase. 'Why on airth did
ye come here at this moment of all times?' Well,
Field took it for granted that it was Lucar who had
come back, and since, so he says, he'd become pretty
fed up with the two of them, he went off home and
left Madrigal to get his other friend to take him along
to a doctor. That is Field's statement, and you may
feel as I did, that it is highly unsatisfactory, but we
mustna forget that Miss Ivory came running from
the yar-rd because she thought there was someone
out in the wee shed down there, and that someone
could not have been Lucar, because of Miss Dorset's
evidence he was accounted for at that time. Still,
Field admits that he handled the hat and coat and
that is highly seegnificant. Field got the hat and
coat out of the lobby across the hall. Noo, anyone
might have seen him do that and this whole story
might have been an invention of his to cover that
conteengency. I can't get it out o' ma heid that the

mur-rderer, whoever he or she was, saw in the absence
of the hat an' coat a remarkably good way to ensure
that the man would not be sairched for in the hoose.
The mur-rderer threw the hat and coat into the
cupboard after the deid man."

"No," said Gabrielle. She was always more alive
at night, and now her fine hard voice was almost
young. "No," she repeated. "Most of what you have
said is excellent, Inspector. I congratulate you. But
on that point you are wrong. I know that because
I put the hat and coat over the poor wretched man
myself."

"You didn't! You didn't! You don't mean it! You
don't know what you're saying!"

Dorothea's outburst shook the room while it still
was tingling, and the soft chatter of the ornate clock,
racing to keep pace with time, was still loud in every
ear. She planted herself before Gabrielle and appealed
directly to the inspector.

"She doesn't know what she's saying. I told you
she'd come out with things she didn't mean. Don't
believe her. Don't you dare believe her."

The very old woman in the wing chair made a
sound. It was a thin, soft tinkle of amusement, as if
a ghost had laughed.

"Dear," she said cajolingly, "my dear, dear
Dorothea, you don't think I killed the poor vulgar
little man, do you? Both of them? I? Sit down. Sit
down, Dorothea. The inspector is doing his puzzle
and I must contribute my piece. I went downstairs
that night. It was my first evening in my old home

and I was restless. Dorothea left me sitting up by the fire and I began to remember all sorts of things, things that had just happened and things that had happened long ago. I was very angry with Robert. He had been very rude to me and I was worried about his attitude towards my girl Frances and that odious little camel man."

Her voice was clear and strong and very graceful, but she glanced up at the clock once or twice and frowned because her sight would not reach it. Bridie did not dare to interrupt her. She had shocked all the blandness out of him, and he stood looking at her as if he expected her to produce a cauldron and broomstick before his eyes.

"I got up and walked about my room first," she said. "I found I was much stronger than I had supposed and it occurred to me that I could move all over the house if I wanted to. God knows I knew it well enough. I made up my mind I'd go down to Robert and talk to him. Until then I had not felt strong enough to give him a serious lecture, but that night, after the quarrel in the afternoon, I felt quite capable of managing him or anyone else, so I went."

She paused and in their minds' eye they saw her, a little bundlesome figure in trailing woollen lace, bobbing lightly over the shining parquet floor.

"It was dark," said Gabrielle, "but I knew every inch of the dear old house and I paused in the hall to listen. It was quite silent, but I saw the garden-room door was open and that there was a light inside, so I went along there."

"God Almighty!" said Withers and shut his mouth with a snap immediately afterwards.

Gabrielle ignored him.

"I pushed open the door a little wider," she said, "and I went in. The blinds were down and at first I thought the room was empty. Then I saw the cupboard door was slightly open."

"Open? Are you sure of that, ma'am?"

Both policemen spoke at once and she glanced up at them disapprovingly.

"Yes, slightly open. I went over and looked inside."

She stopped and shook her head.

"Poor fellow," she said, adding typically, "so undignified and grotesque."

"Did you touch him?"

"I?" Her disdain made Bridie regret his question. "Of course not. It was perfectly obvious that the man was dead. His jaw had dropped. I've seen death too often to mistake it. I went across the room and sat down to think. It was a very awkward situation. I am an old woman. Frances is a young girl, and poor Phillida is a neurasthenic. Obviously none of us was capable of handling the scandal of a police enquiry. There was only one thing to do. I decided that Robert must wait until my son could return to see to things."

She made the outrageous statement with such simple egotism that no one doubted her for an instant. Of course that was what she had done. How exactly like her. In his astonishment Bridie forgot to

look at the clock, while the little hand crept nearer
and nearer to the top of the dial.

"It was then that I saw the hat and coat," Gabrielle continued calmly. "Naturally the idea occurred
to me at once. Since the cupboard was normally
empty presumably it was seldom opened, and if
Robert vanished and his outdoor clothes went with
him no one would look for him in the house. I carried
the heavy coat across to the cupboard and went
back for the hat and gloves. I placed them on his
body quite reverently and then I closed the door,
using my shawl to cover my fingers. I rested for a
little while and then I went back to my room. When
I switched off the light I used my shawl again. I
remember I was quite clearheaded and I arranged
with Dorothea to cable for Meyrick. I did not tell
her about Robert. It seemed to me that the fewer
people there were who knew about it the less morbid
and unpleasant the situation became."

"But what a ghastly secret to keep to yourself all
those days, ma'am!" Bridie was not reproachful so
much as respectful.

Gabrielle met his eyes contemptuously.

"If you had lived when I did, my dear man," she
said bitterly, "you'd have learned how to keep a
great many hard secrets. That is what disgusts me
about this present age. You have no mental discipline. A great many people sneer at the Victorians but
no other period had our *face*."

"I believe you, ma'am," murmured Bridie fervently and would have continued had she not stopped him.

"Wait," she said. "I have not finished yet. Some of your puzzle is filled in, Inspector, but there are several important pieces which remain before we can all see this recognisable portrait you talk about. One of them is this. On the day that poor Robert's body was discovered by the servants the miserable little Lucar rushed away to America. At first the inference to be drawn from that behaviour seemed perfectly obvious to anyone who did not know how long Robert had been in the cupboard, but to me it was quite incomprehensible. If Lucar had killed Robert why had he not run away before? Then, as you have told us, it became apparent that Lucar could not have known of the discovery of the body at the time when he hurried out of the country. That does not explain everything. There remains one of your vital pieces, Inspector. Why did Lucar run away?"

The room was still quiet and Bridie was still looking at her when there came from the hall the sound which brought them all to their feet, their eyes on the clock. It was two minutes to four, and the deep voice in the hall outside was familiar to most of them.

"Meyrick!"

Godolphin limped across the room and met the newcomer as the door swung wide. Meyrick Ivory came in alone, although there was the ominous gleam of silver buttons in the hall behind him. He was a heavy, wide-shouldered man with a shock of white hair and the smooth ruddy face of the squire rather than the Londoner. He kissed his daughter, nodded briefly to the policeman, and hurried to his mother's side.

"Oh, my poor little old girl," he said. "Oh, darling, how are you?"

The old Gabrielle looked up at him with the first sign of tenderness anyone had seen on her face. Her fine thin lips quirked.

"In full command, my boy," she said distinctly. "In full command."

Frances did not hear her. Ever since Bridie had made his dramatic references to the new facilities for air travel an appalling possibility had occurred to her. She glanced at the clock. It was almost four. The hand was within a fraction of the vertical. She looked at Bridie furtively. He was still watching the clock. Even while her eyes rested on him, however, he turned his head and glanced towards the door. It was opening quietly.

Two plain-clothes men appeared first and then, between them, pale and dishevelled, with a portfolio under his arm, came David. He looked round eagerly and, catching her eye, smiled wryly at her.

Gradually they all became aware of him. The babble of voices died abruptly and there was a long silence. Meyrick, standing by his mother's chair, raised his head and stared coldly at the little group. Bridie looked at David.

"Well?" he enquired.

David lifted his eyes, and they saw for the first time how deadly tired he was. He opened his mouth and made the most unexpected and incomprehensible reply.

"It was the one with the smallest moustache," he said.

The senior plain-clothes man nodded his agreement. "As I told you on the phone this morning, sir. We've got five good witnesses, with dates. The depositions are here with the pictures."

Bridie grunted his satisfaction and went over to the table where David had placed the portfolio. Gabrielle leant forward.

"Inspector," she said, "I was asking a very pertinent question. Why did Lucar run away? What else happened on the day that Robert's body was found?"

Her voice cut through the general murmur and every face was turned towards her. Frances, her voice a youthful replica of Gabrielle's own, gave the answer like an echo.

"The papers came out with the news of Godolphin's rescue."

"Yes," said Gabrielle softly. "Godolphin's rescue was announced. That's why Lucar ran away."

"That's an interesting theory but I don't follow it." Godolphin limped forward, his yellow face enquiring. "Why?"

"Chust possibly he was afraid of confr-rontin' you," remarked Bridie from the table. He had unfastened the case and was studying what appeared at a long view to be a large photograph. Suddenly he held it up and they all saw it. It was the head of a Hindu in European clothes but wearing a turban which had been painted on the gloss with process white. He had a little dark moustache, and at first glance the man was definitely Indian. However, there was something uncannily familiar about the attenuated lines of the cheeks and the narrowness of the eyes. Slowly every head in the room save one turned towards Godolphin. The exception was Mrs Sanderson. She remained gaping at the photograph and her triumphant cry shattered the silence, vindicating her obstinacy and airing her insular ignorance in one revealing second.

"The nigger!" she said. "There you are, what did I tell you? That's the nigger I saw."

Godolphin alone remained unimpressed.

"I see someone has been decorating my portrait," he said casually. "That's you, I suppose, Field? Very ingenious, my dear chap, but I don't suppose it proves much, does it?"

"Five people at the Dutch Line Amsterdam Airport recognised it as the passenger arrived there on the day Robert was murdered, and who took the early five o'clock plane out again on the following morning," said David slowly. "I'm sorry, 'Dolly,' but you could have done it in the time."

Godolphin laughed.

"Can any European remember the difference between two Indians?" he enquired lightly.

Bridie did not frown but a shadow passed over his face and he beckoned to Miss Dorset.

"When the Nestor Traders' Protection Association phoned ye chust now in response to your enquiry

what did they tell ye?" he demanded. "Don't be
frightened. Tell it in so many words. Like one or two
other people you became suspeecious when ye discovered that Mr Godolphin, who had left England
penniless, had come home from an unsuccessful ex-
pedeetion with money enough for diamonds and expensive motorcars, so very sensibly ye put the Association on to him. What did ye find out?"

"I found," said Miss Dorset, speaking slowly and
unsteadily, as if the words were forced from her, "I
found that the Bank of India guaranteed him up to
ninety thousand pounds, and—and had done so for
some months on the surety of someone called Habib-
Ul-Raput."

Godolphin whistled. The flippancy struck a false
note, but he was still standing as jauntily as his infirmity would let him in the centre of the hearthrug.

"Partly true," he said. "Raput Habib, of Penang,
is a good friend of mine. I did him a service and he
guaranteed me when I came home. The few months'
story is an extra thrown in by your trade association
friends for luck. Besides, while I admire your combined ingenuity, I'm afraid you're not going to get
my face fitting into your blasted puzzle. Why on
earth should I go to these energetic lengths to kill
Robert in England? Believe me, if I'd wanted to do
the tick in I should have had much more opportunity
in Tibet. Hang it, I saved his life, didn't I?"

"Did you?" In spite of its quietness Gabrielle's
question was menacing. "Did you? When I first
heard that story of your heroism, Mr Godolphin, it

struck me as a plagiarism. When I saw you again,
again I wondered. In my time I have met the kind of
man who sacrifices himself to save his friends, and
he has not been your kind. He has been a great,
simple-hearted, slightly sentimental sort of man, a
hero, a pioneer; if I may use such an old-fashioned
expression, a noble man; but he has never been a
sharp-witted, clever, energetic man like you, Mr
Godolphin. The story of your heroism was the story
that Robert told. It was the kind of slavish imitation
of the real thing which was typical of Robert."

The old voice faded, but as Godolphin bent
towards her she went on again, gathering speed and
strength.

"I wonder if the real story was not more like this?
In the extreme situation which Robert painted far
too vividly for it not to have been true, when you
were a serious burden with your injured leg, when you
had to be carried every step, when the natives
showed dangerous signs of wanting to desert, when
Robert's only support was the miserable Lucar, who
was even more of a physical coward than he himself,
I wonder if then, when you are said to have made
your heroic sacrifice, I wonder if you did nothing of
the kind."

Her voice sank again until they could only just
hear it, a monotone of deadly common sense.

"I wonder if that story was a story of great heroism or a story of great cowardice. I wonder if Robert
left you, Mr Godolphin. I wonder if Robert gave you
a blanket and a tin or two of provisions and left you

screaming to him in the snow. I wonder if he dragged
Lucar on with him and when they returned to safety
remembered the magnificent old story of gallantry
to cover his cowardice. And I wonder if that was the
hold which Lucar had over him, Mr Godolphin."

The man was gaping at her. There were little beads
of sweat on his forehead beneath the line of his
hair.

"Witchcraft," he said, but the laughter which
should have been in the word was not convincing.
"My God, a genuine witch at last! Well, even so,
suppose you're right. Suppose by some misguided
miracle you happen to have hit on something of the
truth. Prove it! Prove he left me. Prove I starved and
froze and rotted for three days before, by the grace
of God, a gang of priests picked me up. Prove I won
their confidence. Prove they nursed me. Prove they
fitted out a new expedition and that I got to Tang
Quing and came back over the pass with enough stuff
to buy old Raput Habib for life. Prove I came to
England with his papers after I had found that
Robert had finished his fine work with a master stroke
and had married Phillida. Prove that with Raput
Habib's help I worked out a cast-iron scheme to pay
him back what I owed him. Prove I hid in a shed in
the yard. Prove I killed him. Prove I killed Lucar
when he practically told the whole lot of you what he
knew. Prove I killed Lucar after he whistled 'Little
Dolly Daydream' to you until he was black in the
face. Little Dolly Godolphin Daydream, the song
that he tortured Robert with until to kill him was an

act of Christian charity. Prove I killed him, Mrs Clairvoyant Gabrielle. What with?"

The man was in a state of ecstasy, drunk with his own words and his own impudent courage. His thin back was straight, his infirmity had disappeared, he used his hands as he talked, and as he finished his stick swung dangerously near her face.

A tiny hand shot out and caught the ferrule, twisting it sharply to the left.

"I've been wondering about this for twenty-four hours. My husband had one," whispered the old Gabrielle, and Godolphin started back from her with two feet of shining swordstick in his hand.

19

THE BEST POLICEMAN IN THE WORLD,
and Bridie privately accredited himself with that dis-
tinction, is not prepared for a conjuring trick at the
psychological moment of arrest.

For the brief part of a second Godolphin was at an
advantage and he took it. He reached the door and
got it open before they leapt on him and Frances
heard for the third time the sharp, quick, purposeful
footsteps which had made such an indelible impression on her mind.

Norris, who was nearest, stuck out a foot to trip
him and received a flick which laid open his upper
arm to the bone for his trouble. The two men on duty
in the hall came for the fugitive with their bare hands,
as their discipline so inconsiderately demands.

The younger, a heavy lout new-recruited from the
Wolds, snatched at the weapon and lost a finger. The
older and more experienced tried a rugby football
tackle but was dodged by a man who knew the game
as well as he did, and Godolphin gained the square.

His fortnight's enforced limping had not impaired
his natural agility and he took the steps lightly.
Petrie, of the *Courier*, might have stopped him, for
he was directly in his path, but he had his own affairs

to attend to and by refraining he obtained one of the finest news photographs of the year and a pictorial scoop for his paper.

It was the crowd who defeated Godolphin, and the symbolism of that defeat was horribly right and just. His sin was against them, and the civilisation which made their existence possible. In a civilised world murder is a crime against the public and the man who commits it is public property, doomed to public justice and public punishment.

When Godolphin appeared on the top of the steps the crowd by the railings opposite were stolidly silent, lost in that state of morbid contemplation which is so incomprehensible to the individual. They were standing dejectedly in the wind and the rain, their eyes fixed hopefully on the dark house across the glistening ribbon of wet asphalt.

No crowd of this type is quick witted, and the wiry figure had cleared the steps and plunged down the pavement towards the lights of St James before they grasped the significance of his appearance. However, the moment one individualist among them came to life and leapt out into the roadway the entire pack was galvanised as by a single electric shock. The roar, which is primitive and hideous and like no other sound in the world, went up from them and they surged in to pursuit.

They never caught him. The Piccadilly traffic did that as he made a wild dash through it to reach, so the papers said afterwards, the car showrooms on the opposite side of the road. The story at the time was

that he was attempting to duck into the doorway
unseen by his pursuers and afterwards to escape in
the car for which he was already negotiating, but
that was only a theory. Whatever the truth was, the
traffic got him. It swept down the greasy road like an
avalanche of red and gold; busses speeding to keep
to schedule, little black taxicabs as mobile as flies on
a ceiling and very like them, three-ton delivery trucks
and a shoal of private cars.

He was dead two seconds after he left the pavement. The two busses shrieked and swayed and
brushed one another in a hail of breaking glass as the
hatless figure rebounded from the radiator of the
first and pitched beneath the double wheels of the
second.

The avalanche was still for a minute or two and the
crowd pressed forward shyly.

.   .   .   .

Frances and David went for a walk that night.

By eleven o'clock 38 Sallet Square was comparatively peaceful. Meyrick and Miss Dorset were still
over at the gallery in conference with the head of the
accounts department. Nurse King was nodding over
a book in Phillida's room. Norris was in the kitchen
nursing his wounded arm and submitting to the
ministrations of Molly and Mrs Sanderson. Gabrielle
lay in her monstrous bed beneath the tapestry and
Matthew, Mark, Luke and John blessed her with
their needlework smiles, while Dorothea muttered
mingled prayers for her deliverance and imprecations

at the fate which should have had the impudence to decree that she should ever have been in any danger.

The walk was David's idea and Frances was grateful to him for it before they had been out of the house ten minutes. Walking is a great sedative and the peace and solidity of an old city at night tends to make personal affairs, however terrible, seem small beside such ancient tranquillity.

The sky had cleared and it was mild, with stars over the spires, and in the air a strange damp exhilaration which is peculiar to London.

They walked along in silence for a long time, heading down the Haymarket to Whitehall and the river. It was quiet once they left the theatre centre, and they walked on wide pavements which they had practically to themselves.

"Poor old 'Dolly,'" David said suddenly. "You can almost forgive him, you know. He had great provocation. And guts too," he added after a pause. "Terrific guts. The Lucar killing needed something like nerve. He must have taken Phillida upstairs and gone straight along to Gabrielle's empty room, walked through the cupboard, done his work and come calmly out again the same way, ambling downstairs to try the Packard. We forgot how well he knew the house. Phillida must have guessed. Did she?"

"I think so." Frances spoke soberly. "I think Gabrielle got it out of her that time she sent the nurse away. I think that's how she knew so certainly. You knew too, didn't you?"

"Yes," he said. "I knew. I knew he'd killed
Robert. I knew that night when we were all at the
Marble Hall. He accused me. Do you remember?
He worked himself up, described the scene, and
suddenly gave himself away by referring to Robert's
grey lock flapping in his eyes. I was so startled that I
thought he'd seen my face. Robert went grey in the
last six months of his life. He told me so. Besides, I
saw it myself. He was bleaching before one's eyes."
He shook his head. "That whistle on the telephone
was a damnable torture of Lucar's. Anyway, as soon
as 'Dolly' mentioned the grey hair I knew that he
was describing a picture that he'd really seen. I
didn't know what to do. I was appallingly sorry for
Phillida and scared stiff generally. It put me on the
idea, of course. I began to work out how he could
have done it, and it was so abominably easy once
one accustomed one's mind to the size of the scheme.
I knew he did speak all these border dialects, and
it dawned on me that if he had somehow got out of
Tibet with something really worth having there was
no reason why he shouldn't have lain low for a bit
while he disposed of the stuff and turned it into cash.
In the course of this he could easily have heard the
story of his own heroic death and Robert's marriage
and have sneaked back into the country, done his
killing and roared back again in time to take part in
a grand resurrection ceremony, the details of which
he had arranged beforehand. There were no Imperial
Airways sailing on the day after the murder, but as
soon as I looked into the Dutch Air Line arrange-

ments the whole thing became staggeringly clear. He could do it in six days."

He paused and shook his head.

"Lucar's return pulled me together," he said, "and as soon as I saw what was going to happen there I knew I must get busy. I was hours and hours too late, of course."

"I saw you," she remarked unexpectedly. "I saw you leave the gallery just as the excitement started. Just as Lucar's body was discovered."

"Did you? That shook the duchess up a bit, didn't it?" He was grinning at her with his old lazy sophistication and she felt comforted. "I'd been down to the framing department. The foreman there has a very fine collection of celebrities pinned up on the wall and I thought he might have a better photograph of Godolphin than the two or three I'd got from the news agency. However, I wasn't lucky and I had to use what I had. It was a simple, rather childish idea. Working on the theory that when Mrs Sanderson said 'nigger' she might easily mean a high-caste Hindu whose ancestors were discussing theology while her own were still leaping from twig to twig, I simply took out my box of paints and decorated half a dozen press photographs of 'Dolly' with various turbans and fancy moustachings. It was hardly a disguise at all. That's why it was so successful. He was quite right when he said what European can tell the difference between two Indians. The ordinary casual observer simply sees a dark chap in a turban. Well, I was in the thick of my art work

when the police came round with the news about
Lucar and started asking a lot of suspiciously intimate questions. I was jittering with terror. I'm no
hero, you know. I spilt every bean I had. I think
they believed me in the end. Old Cholly Good Chob
did anyway, when they brought me round to see him
in the gallery, or he wouldn't have let me go in to
Gabrielle through the cupboard. He was listening
through the door, you know. I think she knew he was
there. However, he wouldn't hear of me going off to
the Dutch airport to verify my theories. That's why
I had to cut and run for it. He wanted to talk to Mrs
Sanderson first. I told him it was too damned dangerous, with 'Dolly' going berserk in the place, and I
think he must have seen that although he didn't
admit it."

"Did they trace you?"

"No, I don't think they even missed me. That was
rather degrading. They knew I'd gone into the house
and presumably hadn't come out. When they did
find I'd gone they broadcast a description, but I
phoned Bridie as soon as I landed at the Amsterdam
Airport, just to be on the safe side, you know. He
sent a couple of men over by the morning plane and
they did the dirty work, interviewing the stewards
and so on. Bridie wasn't certain of his proofs against
'Dolly.' That's why he was waiting to have a show-
down the moment we got back with the deposition.
He seems to have kept you all amused in the meanwhile in his own inimitable way. We were all expect-
ing fireworks, but I didn't envisage anything like

Gabrielle's sensational performance with the swordstick."

Frances shivered.

"That was incredible," she murmured. "As soon
as that had happened the whole thing slid into focus.
Godolphin never let the stick out of his hand, you
see, and as long as one thought he was lame it wasn't
extraordinary. He even had it with him that night he
invented the burglar."

"When Lucar came?"

"Lucar?"

"Oh lord, yes, that was Lucar. Didn't you know?
The police did. 'Dolly' must have had a phone
message from him while we were still at the police
station. It was 'Dolly' who left the yard door open
for him. That's how he got in. He went into the
garden room, opened the cupboard door just to make
sure—you know how one does—pulled a chair up
and was settling down to wait. I imagine he had some
sort of idea of putting the screws on 'Dolly' then.
However, he mucked his entrance. Norris heard him
and ran into 'Dolly' going downstairs. He bunked
and 'Dolly' had to stage the burglary scene by
kicking over the gong. Lucky for Lucar, I should
say."

They had come to the end of the street and he
pulled her arm through his as they crossed the empty
square.

"Where did Godolphin get it?" she said, her mind
running on over the tragedy. "I thought they were
unheard of nowadays."

"Swordsticks? No. That's what I thought, but apparently they're not. I put that question to Withers tonight when he called and he says he's been making enquiries this evening and he finds to his horror that you can buy 'em in every umbrella shop in the city. They cost anything from fifty bob to fifty quid, and the average small branch store still sells about thirty-five a year. It gives one to think, doesn't it? I shall eye every old boy with a malacca with deep respect in future."

They reached the bridge and paused to look over the parapet. Big Ben blinked down on them and the coloured advertisement signs from upriver stained the water below. They remained there for some time and presently David turned his head.

"Well?" he said.

"Well?"

"It's on our minds, isn't it, ducky?"

It was pointless to misunderstand him and she laughed.

"I suppose so."

"What are you going to do? Invest your Poor Mama's Fortune in the Grand Old Firm and bestow yourself on the Lowly But Not Impoverished Painter, setting forth in April for a New World with the Dawn in its Radiance beckoning you to a Fresh and Glowing Love Life?"

Frances considered him. He was abominable.

"You'd have the shock of your existence if I didn't," she said and her eyes were as confidently mocking as his own.